NEVER FORGET THE PAST

A CLEAN ROMANTIC SUSPENSE

LORANA HOOPES

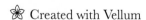 Created with Vellum

To my wonderful readers who inspire me to write everyday.
To Shari who helped me make this the novel it needed to be.
To my writing students who read my first chapter and inspired me
to keep going.

CHAPTER 1

She loved to watch things burn. Fire meant renewal. It allowed the old and useless items to be destroyed so new and worthwhile things could take their places. It was also cleansing. Sins could be erased in fire. The hot, searing heat held perfection and no mercy. No one could escape the fire's wrath. Which was why it had to be done.

Some people believed that God doled out judgement, but the truth was that God was often too merciful. Too full of grace. He forgave people who didn't deserve it. Therein lay the need for His angels. People who could witness the depravity of man or woman and take the necessary steps to cleanse the world. People like her.

She let the match burn to her fingertips, enjoying the

heat that pulsed through her hand. Some angels preferred fancier ways to fulfill their duties. The news was littered with stories of shootings, drownings, some even used drugs, but she had always enjoyed the simplest way. A little gasoline and a match. All it took was an open window, a splash of gas, one strike, and the fire would lick the gas up in giant gulps. Flames would race each other to the top of the house and snake their way along the walls. She never had to be inside this way, but she always made sure they were. And she always struck at night when the blanket of deep sleep would keep them from escaping. So far, no one had escaped.

The match, a charred remnant of wood now, floated to the ground. When it landed, she placed the toe of her shoe over it and twisted, burying it into the dirt. She only ever left one. To leave any more would be tempting fate. Even the one she left was always a way back from the scene, but it was her homage, her thanks for being bestowed with this honor. Not everyone could do what she did, and she willingly bore the weight of her title.

As the flames licked higher, she stepped back into the comforting dark of the forest. The limbs of the trees reached out for her like arms of a mother, and the leaves hid her form so she could watch undisturbed. Watching was her favorite part. She thrived on the fear that graced each face that saw the fire, the terror that colored each voice as they yelled out orders or cried. Even the nervous bustling activity brought a smile to her face. But the best part by far was when the coroner arrived, and the body left the house in its black bag.

A finality existed just in the word black - its heavy feeling on the tongue and its abundance of thick blended consonants - but even more in the form of it. Zipped from head to toe, no more light poked into the bag. No more grace. Only darkness. A shiver of delight ran down her spine at the thought. Yes, that was her favorite part.

She settled against the tree and waited. It had been a long time, but finally, she was back.

CHAPTER 2

*C*aptain Makenna Drake ran a slender hand through her chin-length brown hair as she stared at the charred remains of a house - her crime scene - and sighed. It had been so quiet the last few years. Why did this have to start again now?

"Do you think it's the same guy?" Tad asked from behind her shoulder.

She glanced up at her lieutenant, the only other cop still on the force who had worked the murder case five years ago. He'd been young then, fresh out of the academy and eager to learn even though he had spent more time typing reports and fetching coffee than he had processing evidence. He was older now, but his face still boasted his youth. It was not yet marred with the wrinkles the stress of this job brought, but it would be if he stayed a cop much longer.

It happened to them all, she supposed. Death would come across their paths and leave his mark - a graying of the hair here, a few wrinkles there, the inability to process emotions or maintain healthy relationships sprinkled in for good measure. She had seen it before with her first captain. Fierce and stoic, he had been a force to reckon with - hard to please and even harder to earn praise from. But he'd been unhappy. After two divorces and little contact with the children who had written him out of their lives years ago, drinking had become his companion. First, a little nip here and there when an especially tough case crossed their desks - the death of a child, physical abuse, or the like. But then she'd noticed it more often - the frequent trips to his office, the darker mood, the sallow complexion.

And so she had transferred to a smaller department. Convinced that the crime of the bigger city had been his downfall, she'd chosen a smaller town with a lower crime rate, but she found the same markers here. Sure, it took longer, but the aging still happened. Her superiors both looked a decade older than they were. The captain had recently filed for divorce and the sergeant's relationship was hanging on by a thread, but she would be different. She'd promised herself she would find time to date, that

she would leave her work at work and fully engage at
home, but she hadn't.

And then one day, she'd seen the toll in her own
mirror - the bags under her eyes where there had
previously been none and the coarse gray hairs that
contrasted with her dark hair - both in color and in
manageability.

Tad's hair held no traces of that gray yet, and his
eyes glistened with curiosity and wonder - something she
had lost long ago. But he hadn't been entrenched in the
previous case the way she had. And life had returned to
normal after the last death - traffic stops and bar brawls,
but nothing serious. She wondered if he would still look
so young when this was over, or if, like her, his face
would bear the brunt of the weight of cases like this.

"I don't know if it's the same guy," she said,
returning her gaze to the blackened structure. "The MO
is the same. House fire at night, open or broken window
where the fire starts, but all the victims last time were
women."

"Except for Matt Fisher," he said.

Right, Matt Fisher. The final victim. The man
everyone thought was dead. Everyone except Makenna
who knew better. Everyone except Makenna who sent
him away when he came to her after the attempt on his
life. "Yes, except for him." She forced her face to remain
impassive. Tad didn't know what she had done, and she

wasn't sure she was ready to tell him yet. "But if our killer changed his victim MO with Matt, why the long break?"

Confusion clouded Tad's face, dimming the brightness of his eyes momentarily, and he shook his head. "Something must have triggered him."

"Yes, but what?" Makenna hated that this guy was killing again. She hated the fear that would blanket the small town as it had five years ago. She hated the fact that she hadn't caught the guy last time. Even more, she hated the fact that she had told Matt Fisher to leave, had let his family believe he was dead, for nothing. She'd thought she was saving him, had thought the killer was after him, but now he was striking again even though Matt Fisher was long gone. How much of Matt Fisher's life had she destroyed with her wrong choice?

She supposed it could be a copycat. The fires always started at night when the victims were asleep. They always started inside an open window, and the only accelerant they could ever determine was gasoline. Sometimes the window was broken, but they never found fingerprints or what he used to break it which meant he took the item with him and probably wore gloves. It wasn't much to go on, but it was possible someone had read about the old cases and decided to try his hand. It certainly wouldn't be hard to copy.

Makenna didn't think so though. Woodville was a

smaller town - not tiny but small enough that violent crimes were few and far between. Most of her time was spent ticketing speeders or the occasional red light runners. Besides those murders five years ago, the only other big case they'd had was when Tommy Granger went missing for a few hours and his parents believed he'd been kidnapped. Turned out, he had fallen asleep in the dog house with their new puppy and just didn't hear all the shouts.

So, the chances of a copycat choosing their town again just didn't sit right with her. It made much more sense that something had appeased the killer last time and something had triggered him again this time. Of course, the only thing that could have appeased him last time was the death of Matt Fisher, but then why start killing again? As far as Makenna knew, she was the only one who knew Matt was alive, who knew where he was. Had there been more to it last time? Something she had missed?

"What are we going to do, Captain?" Tad asked.

Makenna took another deep breath and uttered the words she'd both hoped and dreaded to say. "I guess I'm going to bring someone back from the dead."

*B*illy "Bubba" Campbell glanced around his apartment as he locked up. Though he enjoyed his alone time, he wished he had someone to share the evenings with, but his job as a firefighter kept him busy. And then there was the issue with his past. No one in Fire Beach knew his real past, and though he had fully embraced his current life, that reality made it hard to let people in - really in - enough to form a relationship with. Besides, what if it happened again? He couldn't stand any woman he cared about getting hurt again. No, it was better this way. He would just be content with good friends and the good Lord.

Speaking of good friends, he better hurry up. Tonight, Detective Jordan Graves, was throwing a party for Tia Sweetchild, the author who had ended up in their town after a car accident the opening night of Jordan's restaurant. They had all worked to save her, and though she'd had a long recovery, she'd done it with the help of her now-boyfriend, Dr. Brody Cavanaugh. Bubba still marveled at how the members of the different departments had bonded.

The rest of the crew was already at the restaurant when Bubba entered, but thankfully, his friend and fellow firefighter Luca had saved him a seat. Luca was a Southerner like Bubba, but Bubba had quickly learned after meeting Luca that there were two types of

Southerners. There were southerners from Texas like he was - people who said ya'll, loved okra, and called every drink a coke. And then there were the people from the deep south, like Luca who was from Georgia. The differences were few, but they came out occasionally, usually around food. Bubba still remembered the time Luca had called him a Yankee for not knowing what a ham hock was. Weird that they now both lived up North in Illinois.

He slid into the seat next to Luca just as Jordan tapped his water glass with a spoon. Though he would never have opted for the title, Jordan had become their representative, their glue. His commanding presence was a large part of that - he had a natural ability to draw the attention when he walked into a room. Couple that with his occupation as a cop as well as the co-owner of the restaurant, and he was in the forefront quite often.

The conversation quieted, allowing him to speak. "Thank you all for coming. As you know, we have a resident celebrity in our midst." He smiled at Tia, and she dropped her eyes as a soft pink color crawled up her cheeks. "And she has finally finished her masterpiece. Tia get up here and show off your beautiful book." Tia had been an author before her accident, but after it, she had taken some time to work in the restaurant while she healed. Somehow, she had managed to write a book at the same time.

Tia shook her head as she pushed back her chair. Bubba didn't know all of Tia's story, but he'd heard a little through the grapevine and he'd been there when she had first been rescued with the Jaws of Life. It would be hard to tell she had ever been in a serious accident except for the large red scar that still arced across her forehead.

She grabbed a bag and walked to the front of the table. "Thank you all for wanting to celebrate this with me. This wasn't an easy book to write, but your support helped me get past all the hard parts. Now, I've loved a lot of books I've written, but I think this might be my best."

"Hear, hear," Brody, her boyfriend and ICU doctor, said lifting his glass and flashing her a large smile. "What?" he asked as he looked around the table. "I already read it, so I know that it's good. She got the doctor spot on."

Tia shook her head and smiled at him. "Anyway, I think it is because of all of you that it turned out so well, and that's why I'm pleased to present to you…" she paused before pulling the book out of the bag, "The Key to Remember."

Bubba joined in the cheers and clapping as Tia passed the book around the table. He hadn't read it yet, but if it chronicled her narrow escape from the men who had been after her when she lost her memory, he had no doubt it would be interesting. When the book reached his hands, he flipped through the pages before turning to Luca Sanders. "Hey, this might even be a book you could read, Luca."

"Only if it's on audiobook," Luca shot back. "I can't sit still long enough to read a paper book. Sorry, Tia."

"You probably couldn't focus long enough to listen to an audiobook either," Bubba said with a deep chuckle. "Unless maybe it was a Dr. Seuss book."

"Hey, there is nothing wrong with Dr. Seuss," Luca said, punching Bubba in the arm. "I still remember Green Eggs and Ham. Of course, maybe that's because our teacher actually made us eat green eggs." A grimace contorted his face and Bubba laughed out loud.

"Excuse me?"

The conversation stilled at the unfamiliar voice, and Bubba's blood ran cold. It couldn't be. She'd promised not to come find him unless the murders started again. He turned toward the doorway where a petite woman stood. She was thinner and her hair held a few more silver strands, but Bubba would have wagered a year's wage that the woman was Makenna Drake.

"I'm sorry to interrupt, but do any of you know where I can find Matt Fisher?" Her eyes scanned the room, and Bubba knew when they reached him, she would recognize him. He hadn't changed that much in five years. They hadn't thought a change of appearance would be necessary. Moving him a few hours away and giving him a whole new name and past had seemed like enough, especially since Makenna hadn't known the name he'd chosen. She had set him up with a hacker she knew who could arrange a new identity complete with documents. She'd agreed to know the town he moved to in case she needed to find him again, but she hadn't wanted any more knowledge in case the killer ever realized they had faked Matt's death and went after Makenna for information.

Confused glances shot around the room and Jordan stood to address her. "I'm sorry, ma'am, there's no Matt Fisher here."

"Actually, there is." Bubba took a deep breath and let it out in a sigh. Time seemed to freeze as every eye turned his direction, and he pushed back his chair and stood. "I'm Matt Fisher."

"What? What are you talking about, Bubba? Who is this woman?" The questions fired at him from all across the table and Bubba held up his hands to quiet them down.

"I'll answer all your questions, but let me start with the last one first." He turned to Makenna and motioned her to join them. "This is Lieutenant Makenna Drake."

"Actually, it's Captain now."

Bubba raised a brow and shot her a glance riddled with questions. She was a good cop, but captain already?

She smiled and shrugged as if reading his mind. "It's a small town."

He chuckled at that. "It is, but somehow I doubt that's the only reason you're a captain now. I should have expected nothing less." He looked away from Makenna and back to his friends to continue his story. "Captain," he emphasized the word, "Drake is from Woodville where I used to live."

"Woodville? I thought you were from Texas," Luca said.

"I am originally from Texas, but I moved to Woodville in high school. I graduated there and trained to become a firefighter."

"You? Or Matt Fisher?" Jordan asked, and Bubba did not miss the note of suspicion threading his voice.

"Matt Fisher. That is the name I was born with. Anyway, for a couple of years, it was great. I loved the area and my job, but then about five years ago, people began dying."

"Women, specifically," Makenna said, joining in. "Women who happened to die in fires and all had some connection to Matt."

"You didn't honestly think he was responsible, did you?" Cassidy asked. Daggers flew from her eyes and laced her voice.

Bubba had to smile at Cassidy. She was the only female firefighter in their unit, and she was like his little sister. He was fiercely protective of her, and it appeared she was of him as well.

"We didn't have much to go on," Makenna said sadly. "Nothing is ever left at the scene, and the only link seemed to be Matt."

"So, what changed your mind?" Officer Alayna "Al" Parker asked.

"When I became a victim," Bubba said. "Maybe it was because I'm always around fires, but the smell woke me up, and I escaped. Makenna decided then that I wasn't the perpetrator and that it would be safer if I left town and changed my name. She helped me set up this new identity. I didn't mean to lie to you all." Bubba meant every word, but he also couldn't deny feeling lighter finally sharing his past with his friends.

"That all makes sense," Jordan said, "but why are you back now?"

Makenna bit her lip and then sighed as she caught Bubba's eye. "Because the murders have started again."

Bubba's heart sank at the words, and a seed of anger sprouted in his chest. Makenna had told him that whoever was behind the killings held a vendetta against him for some reason and would stop with the news of his death. He had believed her. He had let his family believe he was dead and broken all communication with them. And for what? Nothing, it appeared now.

"I know you have no reason to come back, but I'm

hoping that you will. You were the only victim who survived, though the killer doesn't know that. I'm hoping that seeing that you survived might fluster him enough to mess up and give us some clue as to who he is."

Bubba leaned back as he thought about her request. He owed her nothing. He'd spent the last five years trying to put Woodville out of his mind, to pretend he didn't miss his family. And he was happy here in Fire Beach, mostly. But there had always been that nagging thought in his head. The thought that wondered if he would really ever forget Matt Fisher and truly be Billy Campbell. The thought that the killer had some connection to him and by running, he had put more people in danger.

"I'll do it," he said finally. The thought of going back to Woodville held a sense of relief along with a feeling of terror, but it also felt right.

"Are you sure, Bubba?" Cassidy asked. "It sounds dangerous. Maybe Jordan should go with you." She looked to her boyfriend, but his face was impassive.

"I'm about out of leave, but I'll check with Stone and see if he'll give me some more leave."

"I could go," Al said. "I'm pretty certain I have some leave saved up."

"Guys, I'll be fine," Bubba said, though inside he wondered if that were true. He'd gone through a lot of counseling after leaving Woodville. He'd spent an abundant amount of time trying to forget the women who were killed, trying to forget his family. Could he really go back and relive it all again? What would his parents say?

"Thank you, Matt. I guess it's settled then," Makenna said.

But it didn't feel settled to Bubba. Could he really face his old demons? What if he didn't make it back this time? No, that was out of his hands. God had protected him last time, and He would do it again this time if it was His will. Bubba shook his head to clear the voices and turned to Makenna. "When do we leave?"

CHAPTER 3

Makenna felt like a trespasser as she stood in Matt's apartment waiting for him to gather some items. She had told him to pack for a week, but what if it turned out to be longer? What if Matt wasn't the link and seeing him did nothing? What if it really was a copycat who would have little knowledge of Matt Fisher at all? Then she would have disrupted his life for nothing.

Trust. She had to trust God that this was the right move. She'd learned to trust her instincts when she became a cop, and they had rarely proved her wrong. But, she knew that trusting God was even more important, and she felt sure He'd led her back to Matt Fisher.

She'd begun looking to God after the case from five

years ago. She'd needed a way to deal with her anger and frustration at not finding the killer. Then, the promotions had happened and stress had consumed her life. Church and her time with God had been the only sanity-saving times for a while.

"Almost ready," he called from the bedroom.

His place was small - a one bedroom apartment, but he had decorated it tastefully. The furniture matched, and the pictures on the wall complemented them. She wondered if he had decorated the place himself or if a woman had?

There had been several women at the restaurant where she'd found him, but none of them appeared to be more than a friend, and she saw no sign of a woman living in the apartment. Of course, it was none of her business if he did have a woman, but for some reason the thought that he didn't... affected her. She told herself it was simply because she too was single and she liked the validation that it was okay to be in your thirties and still single, but if she were honest with herself, she would acknowledge that Matt had a place in her heart.

She had truly believed sending him away was saving not only his life but the lives of his family and friends, but she had never forgotten him. She'd thought often of checking up on him to see how he was doing, but she hadn't wanted to chance the killer finding out he was still alive and coming after him. Now, here he was back in her life. As strong and handsome as he had been five years ago.

"You ready?" he asked.

His voice shook her back to reality, and she nodded. "Do you have anyone to look after the place while you're gone?" It was a cowardly way to ask, but his answer would tell her if he was seeing someone or not.

"Cassidy and Luca both offered to check in on the place."

Makenna nodded and stepped out the front door. "They seem nice. Your friends."

"They are. And protective. They're all I've had for the last five years." She heard no condemnation in his voice, but she felt it all the same - a tiny tug on the invisible chain she wore around her neck.

"I'm sorry, Matt." She hated those words. They sounded trite and empty, but what could she say? There was no manual for situations like this, no course taught at the academy. Even the previous cases she had handled had never forced her to fake a death and destroy a family.

He held up a hand and shook his head. "Let's not rehash the past. You did what you thought was right, and I went along with it. Let's just hope it ends differently this time."

Makenna nodded. What could she say to that? He locked the front door and followed her to her car, but the tension lay heavy between them. Like an unseen barrier. She hoped she hadn't made a mistake coming back here and upending his life. Again.

She turned the key and let the hum of the engine break the silence for a moment. Then she shifted the gear into drive and pulled away. Her fingers tapped against the steering wheel - her nervous gesture - and she searched her mind for anything to say.

"There's a radio," she said, tapping the button on the console. "You can turn it to whatever you want. The country station comes in super clear, but the other ones are a little finicky." She was rambling, but she couldn't seem to keep the words from falling out of her mouth.

"I don't need music, Makenna."

"Right. Sorry." What was she thinking? Of course he didn't need music. He probably needed to process, but why did he seem so comfortable with the silence while it ate her alive?

Although maybe he wasn't comfortable. His posture was so stiff that it looked as if a metal rod had replaced his spine, and his eyes stared vacantly out the window. She wished that she could see what was going on in his head. Was he scared? Nervous? He certainly had every right to be. She sure was. It had been a nightmare working this case five years ago, but she'd still been learning then. Now, she was running the department which meant that more responsibility lay on her shoulders. She had to catch this guy.

"Why Bubba?" she asked. The sound of her voice surprised her. She had been wondering about the nickname from the moment she heard it, but she hadn't meant to ask the question aloud. At least, not yet.

Matt shrugged and turned his head slowly in her direction. "Bubba seemed to fit the Southern personality I had created. Once I said it out loud, it just sort of stuck."

"Should I call you that?" Makenna wasn't sure what to call him. She knew him as Matt, but she also knew he'd been living under a different name for the last few years. How odd must that be? She didn't even like nicknames though her old captain had called her Mac. He was the only one though.

Matt appeared to think for a minute as the knuckles of his right hand ran down the side of his square jaw. She'd forgotten how solid he was, but now that he was in her car, it was hard not to notice how his broad shoulders filled every inch of the passenger seat and how the seatbelt accentuated his muscular chest.

"Yeah, Bubba would be nice. It's the only name that's felt right since I quit being Matt."

"Was it hard to adjust?"

The seatbelt groaned as it stretched with his deep

breath. "It was at first. Especially leaving my life behind. How is my family anyway?"

"They're fine," Makenna said, careful to keep her voice even, but she knew that was far from the truth. His parents had been devastated by Matt's "death," and the grief had aged them faster than they might have without it. She knew he probably had other siblings, but the only one she had ever met was Felicity, his sister who worked for a local doctor. She had grieved briefly, but then she had seemed to continue on as if nothing had happened. Perhaps, it was because of her job. Maybe her boss had given her counseling, but it had still given Makenna pause. His parents, however, would probably be overjoyed to see him now and know he was alive, but Makenna knew they would rain fire down on her for the lie, even if it had been a lie to keep him safe.

"That was the hardest part," he continued. Makenna breathed a sigh of relief that he hadn't pressed about his family any further. "Not seeing my family and learning to respond to a different name. It's not something I ever thought I would have to do, and I wouldn't wish it on anyone. I often felt like I was developing multiple personalities."

Makenna could understand that. Even though she knew he was the same person, the man sitting next to her was different from the one who had left five years ago. His voice was softer. His eyes carried a little more sadness. Even some of his mannerisms seemed different.

"I'm sorry. I thought it was the best way to keep you safe." She hated that she kept apologizing - it made the words sound trite - but what else could she say?

He shrugged again and turned his face back to the window. "It probably was."

Silence filled the car, and Makenna forced her mouth shut. She wanted to ask him more questions. About the last few years, about what he remembered from the previous case, about how he was feeling, but she could tell he wasn't ready to throw that door wide open yet.

"Why do you think he started again?" Matt asked as he turned to her suddenly. No, not Matt. Bubba. He wanted her to call him Bubba, and she would try and honor that. The name felt weird in her head and she imagined it would on her tongue as well, but she would bury her discomfort for him. She owed him that much.

Makenna shook her head but kept her gaze focused on the road in front of her. "I'm not sure. Something definitely triggered him. Maybe a death." She paused, unsure if she should tell him the rest of the issue now or when they could look over the evidence.

"What aren't you saying?"

Her eyes flicked from the road to meet his steely gaze. Now, it was. If he hadn't become a firefighter, he would have made a great cop. "Something in the MO changed."

"A copycat?" Bubba asked.

Makenna shook her head. "No, we're pretty sure it's the same guy. Same details. Fire started at an open window, gas for accelerant, single match found at the scene. Details we never released to the public."

"So, what's changed?"

"The victim. When he struck five years ago, all the victims were women. Except for you. Our current victim is another man."

"What does that mean?" Bubba asked as he shook his head.

"We don't know. We're hoping maybe you can help us figure that out."

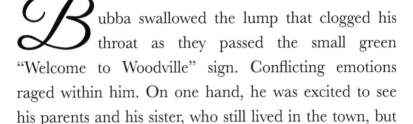

*B*ubba swallowed the lump that clogged his throat as they passed the small green "Welcome to Woodville" sign. Conflicting emotions raged within him. On one hand, he was excited to see his parents and his sister, who still lived in the town, but coming back here also brought back a flood of memories.

Bubba's eyes snapped open. For a second, he wasn't sure what had woken him, but then the odor hit his nose - the acrid smell of smoke. Light but definitely there. Once you've been in a burning building, the smell of the smoke never leaves you, and he had been in enough buildings to never mistake the scent no matter how faint it was. Then the soft crackle of the fire met his ears. He threw his covers back and could already feel the gentle tease of the approaching heat. Out! He had to get out.

He touched the handle of his door and quickly pulled his hand back. An intense heat coated the metal. The fire was right outside of the door then. No opening the door to make it to an exit. No using his fire extinguisher to tame the fire. The idea of losing his house and belongings was sobering. Pictures of his family had been hung around the living room, and his favorite Toby Mac CD was probably melted into the coffee table his parents had bought for him when he first moved out. Even his computer, the Mac he had saved the last few paychecks to get, would be a puddle of melted plastic and metal, but they were just things. As much as he would miss them, things could be replaced, but he hadn't started this fire. Someone else had. Someone who could be the same arsonist who had killed three women in fires recently. Someone who could still be around - watching, waiting to see if Bubba escaped. From his years in the department, Bubba knew many arsonists liked to stay and watch the fires.

Bubba turned from the door and scanned his room. There wasn't time to take much, but he could grab his cell phone and a pair of shoes. No need to destroy his feet as he climbed out of the window or ran to safety. Safety. Could the killer be out there? Waiting for him to open the window? He crossed to the window *and peered into the darkness but saw no one waiting in the immediate vicinity. Still, what if the killer was waiting outside? He could be lurking in the shadows of the large oak tree. Just waiting and watching to make sure Bubba didn't escape. He should have trimmed the tree or better yet removed it altogether, but how could he have known?*

It didn't matter if the killer was out there. It was a chance he had to take. At least outside, he had a possibility of escape. If he stayed in this room, the smoke would choke him, and the fire would eat him alive. And he had no desire to become the fire's victim.

He grabbed his cell phone and threw on a pair of shoes, and then he opened the window and knocked out the screen. It would be a tight squeeze for his large frame, but he thought he would just fit.

The cool night air sent a shiver down his back as it dispelled the heat he had felt just moments before. He should have grabbed a shirt too or a jacket. His feet hit the ground, and he stepped back. The fire had already claimed half of his house, and the flames licked closer to where he stood. With a final glance around him, Bubba shot off in the direction farthest from the fire's origin. Only when he felt he was far enough away not to be seen or heard did he pull his cell phone out and dial 911.

Bubba squeezed his eyes shut to dispel the images of the past and then took a deep breath. He could do this.

"You okay?" Makenna asked beside him.

"Yeah, just dealing with a few old demons."

She didn't press the issue for which Bubba was glad. He didn't want to relive the nightmare out loud. He'd done enough of that in counseling when he'd first moved to Fire Beach. The therapist had been cleared and sworn to secrecy, but Bubba had still been relieved when the sessions ended.

"I know you want to see your family, but I have a feeling it might be a long and emotional reunion, so do you mind if we hit the station first? I want to see what we've found out about our victim."

"Fine." Bubba did want to see his parents and his sister, but he was nervous about it as well. He wouldn't mind the extra time to prepare himself mentally. "Is anybody else from the old case still here?" An unspoken code existed among departments, and so even when he had been a suspect, most of the cops had treated him with respect, but there'd been one, an older, gruff man who had glared at Bubba every time he'd come around.

"Just Tad Brewer. You might not even remember him because he was so new back then, but he's my lieutenant now. Everyone else either retired or took a position in another town."

"Couldn't handle the pressure of the investigation?" Bubba asked.

She glanced at him as she pulled into the parking lot. "I'm sure that was the issue for a few of them - the ones who have always tied everything up with a nice bow. For the others," she shrugged, "I think they thought a small town would be less work."

Bubba chuckled at that, but he bet she was right. Fire Beach couldn't really be classified as a small town, but he had known a few people who had joined the fire department thinking it would be easy money only to find out they stayed relatively busy. Not Chicago busy, but not slow either.

"You ready?" she asked as she turned off the engine.

"As I'll ever be, I guess." Could one ever be ready for something like this? To step back into the fire after narrowly escaping with his life? What if the killer found out he was still alive and went after him again? No. Trust. He had to trust. He whispered a silent prayer as he put his hand on the door.

"Okay, let's go."

CHAPTER 4

*M*akenna pulled open the door and stepped inside the small station first, but she could feel the hulking presence of Bubba behind her. Had he always been such a presence? She remembered him being handsome back then, but she'd been too focused on her career to notice many men. Plus, he'd been a suspect at first, making him unsuitable to date, but now she was settled and he was cleared. And she couldn't deny that he was attractive.

"Hey, Captain," Clark, her newest recruit, said from the front desk. He had just graduated from the academy and was greener than she would have liked, but he seemed like a good kid. Eagerness and a willingness to learn were his best traits, and she would take those over a knowledgeable curmudgeon any day.

"Clark." She nodded at him before continuing through to the evidence room. Tad, Kelsey, and Brayden sat at their respective desks, but all looked up as they entered.

"Guys, this is Matt Fisher, er Bubba, the guy I was telling you about. He's the only one to escape the arsonist, and he's offered to lend whatever help he can. Bubba, you might remember Tad Brewer." She pointed to the dark haired lieutenant before turning to her other two officers. "This is Kelsey Knight and Brayden Cook."

Tad stood first and extended a hand. "Good to see you again, man." The two men shook and then Kelsey stood and threw out her hand as well.

Kelsey had been the first one hired after Makenna's predecessor, Stillman, had made captain. She was good, thorough, and though her thinner frame mislead people, she was tough as nails. Her blond hair was pulled back in its customary ponytail, and her face was nearly devoid of makeup. Still young, she could pull it off, and there were days when Makenna envied that fresh face.

"Nice to meet you, Bubba. Wish it was under better circumstances."

"As do I."

Brayden was the last to stand. He'd sent his application in right after the arsonist story made the news. Makenna hadn't been sure whether he was simply chasing the story or if he was hoping to be the one to break the case. He was tall and lanky, and he had an ego the size of Texas. Had it been her decision, she might not have hired him, but he had turned out to be a decent cop.

"Welcome, Bubba."

"Okay, now that introductions are made, let's catch Bubba up on the case. As you remember, there were three women killed the first time." Makenna moved over to the board where pictures were hanging. She pointed first to the young, perky blond. "Daisy Johnson who worked at the coffee shop you stopped at regularly." Her hand moved to the stunning brunette. "Alexis Gibbons who worked out at the same gym you did, and," her finger moved one more time to the final picture, a pretty redhead with a dusting of freckles across her nose, "Clarissa Wiggins who was a massage therapist and whom you dated briefly, am I right?"

Bubba nodded, but his eyes were wide as he looked from one woman to the next. "When you lay it out like that, I can see why you thought I was a suspect."

Makenna nodded. "You were the only link we could find between these three women. Clarissa and Daisy didn't attend the same gym Alexis did. Neither Alexis nor Clarissa drank much coffee, and we found no record that Daisy or Alexis were ever clients of Clarissa."

"So, if the killer was after me, why go after these women? I barely knew Daisy. I mean I spoke to her the mornings I ordered coffee, but I'd never seen her outside of the coffee shop, and Alexis led the aerobics classes at my gym which I didn't take. The only one I had a true connection with was Clarissa, and we broke up months before she was killed. And it was amicable."

"That's what we've been trying to figure out," Tad spoke up and joined Makenna at the board. "At first we thought the killer was a spurned interest or something. All of these women are beautiful, so perhaps he tried to ask them out and was rejected. That made sense until the attempt on your life."

"When you were brought into the equation, we were left with two scenarios," Makenna continued. "Either the killer wanted to hurt you and he chose these women because he thought they meant something to you or you represented what he would never be."

"But if it were the latter, wouldn't he have kept killing even after me?" Bubba's eyes flicked from Tad to Makenna. "You said the killings stopped after the attempt on my life."

"They did. Until the other night. Now, we have another victim." She motioned to Kelsey who stood and took her place at the board.

"This is Peter Smith," Kelsey said pointing to a picture of a young looking man. "Single though we believe he had a girlfriend. He owned a repair shop on Fifth that he opened a few years ago. There's only one other employee, and we're still working on his friends, but his parents live here as well."

Bubba's brow creased as he gazed at the man. "I don't understand. I don't know that man, and he isn't in the same occupation that I am. Does the killer want to be both of us?"

Makenna exchanged glances with her team. Bubba not knowing Peter did blow a hole in the first theory, and he was right - the other man didn't look like him. He was smaller, more average looking, and his job didn't hold the clout that a firefighter's did. "We don't know."

She hated saying those words. She was supposed to be in control here, but this guy - if it was the same guy and not a copycat - just made no sense. Why the shift in victims? Why the long break? Why did he start killing again? There had to be some connection, some trigger, but she had no idea what it was.

Before she could say more, the door to the room opened and Natasha Kingston, head reporter for the Woodville Gazette and a pure pain in Makenna's backside, burst into the room. "Oh, my word, it is true."

Clark entered behind her, chagrined and apologetic. "Sorry, Captain, she blew right past me."

"It's fine, Clark." Makenna had dealt with Natasha enough to know the woman took pushy to a whole new level. Clark would have been no match for her. "What can I do for you, Natasha?"

Her bright red lips pursed as her eyes shifted from one person to the next until they finally landed on Bubba. "I thought Old Henry was yanking my chain when he burst into my office stating he had just seen a ghost. I almost wrote him off. I am in the middle of a big story, you know, but my back was aching, and I figured I could use a break. So, I decided I would see if there was any truth to the ghost of Matt Fisher getting out of your squad car and entering the building. Boy, am I glad I did."

Makenna rolled her eyes and stifled a sigh as Natasha pulled a portable recorder out of her purse and stepped toward Bubba. "Matt, do you want to tell me your story? I'd be delighted to write an exclusive on you."

Disgust erupted in Makenna's throat at the words that sounded more like a seductive purr than an actual question. While she wanted word to get out about Matt's return, Natasha would not have been her choice.

"Natasha, Matt just got to town. He hasn't even gotten the chance to see his family. Perhaps your exclusive could wait until tomorrow?"

Natasha turned to Makenna, a fake smile plastered on her face. "Captain Drake, it is my job to deliver the news to the good people of Woodville, and this is definitely news. Now, I could run yet another story on how the police department has yet to find the killer who is terrorizing our town after a five year hiatus, or," she turned back to Bubba, "you could give me a few minutes with our former hero here, and I could put out a much nicer piece."

Makenna forced herself to remain calm. Natasha was a dislikeable person, but she was just doing her job. Still, she didn't like the thought of Bubba being subjected to her, especially on his first day back before he'd even had the chance to reunite with his family. She looked to Bubba and shrugged. "I'll leave the decision up to him. We're done here for the day anyway."

Natasha's lips morphed into a sultry pout, and she placed a hand on Bubba's arm. "What do you say, Matt? Can I have a few minutes of your time?"

Though the desire to say no was written all over his face and evident in his posture, Bubba nodded. "Sure, I can give you a few minutes. On one condition."

"What's that?"

"You don't run the story until tomorrow. I want to talk to my folks before they read it in the paper."

Her lips pursed as she appeared to think over the offer. It was early afternoon, and Makenna thought Natasha could get a paper out tonight if she busted her butt, but did she want to work that hard? Besides, evening papers were a rarity in Woodville and most people wouldn't read it until the following morning anyway.

"Fine. I promise not to print it until tomorrow."

"Then you have yourself a deal."

Makenna wanted to apologize for putting Bubba on the spot, but there was no chance to get him alone during the short walk down the hall to one of the conference rooms. She waited in the door frame for an invitation to sit in, but when he didn't offer one, she took the hint and closed the door. He was an adult, and he could take care of himself. So, why did she hate the thought of leaving him alone with Natasha?

*B*ubba settled in his seat and leaned back. He was familiar with Natasha and knew that for the next few minutes, he would need to choose his words carefully. She was a good journalist, but like most, she tended to focus on the words that would make her story pop and bury the rest, even if it ended up twisting the meaning of the interviewee. Thankfully, he had avoided most situations with her when he worked at the firehouse, but he'd heard his captain complain more than once when what she printed took his words out of context.

"So, Matt, why did you let everyone here think you were dead five years ago? Were you hiding something?"

"On the contrary. After the attempt on my life,

Captain Drake and I thought my "death" might keep the killer from going after my family."

"Really? You left your job as a fireman, deserted basically, and you want us to believe you did it to save your family? You were a suspect originally, am I right?"

Bubba didn't like where this was going, and he knew the spin on it would do nothing for his image. He didn't care so much about that as he did about the backlash that would fall on his parents. They'd probably already had to deal with questions and pitying looks and apologies for the last five years, he didn't want any more grief put on them.

He leaned forward and stared into Natasha's eyes. She was tough, but he was tougher, bigger, and had much more at stake. "I know you want a sensational story, Natasha, but that is the truth."

"Perhaps it is." Confidence flowed out of her voice, and her steely eyes never wavered. "But I find it odd that you were the main suspect until your house caught fire. And then after your "death," the fires stopped. Don't you find that a little coincidental?"

"I might. If I were you, and if they hadn't started back up again. What's your spin on that, Natasha? I was hundreds of miles away when this latest one happened."

She smiled, but it was not a warm, friendly smile, more the smile of a predator searching for her next meal. "I think there are two possibilities. Either, you came back early and wanted us to think you were still wherever you've been hiding, so that you would have an alibi. Or you have someone here you've been in contact with doing your dirty work."

Bubba shook his head and leaned away from her. "You have quite the imagination, Natasha, but why don't you try this one on. Imagine that you were the subject of a murder investigation even though you had dedicated your life to saving people. Imagine waking up to the smell of smoke and knowing that everything you own will soon be a pile of black ash. Imagine that you are told the only way to save the ones you love is to leave them forever, never communicate with them, and try to pretend they never existed. Imagine having to move to a new town with a name you've never been called, with a past not your own and try to fit in."

He pushed back his chair and stood up. "And if you finish that and still think you should write the story in your head, then I want you to think about your parents. Think about them mourning you for five years and having to deal with questions and stares from the neighbors and people they once called friends. Imagine their joy when they realize you're alive and then their utter destruction when someone fabricates a story about you and calls it news simply because they can."

Her mouth opened, but Bubba had no intention of letting her have the last word. "You can write whatever story you want, Natasha, but God help your soul if you write the trash you can't back up with facts and pretend it's truth."

With that he walked out of the room and found himself face to face with an embarrassed Makenna.

"I'm sorry, I didn't mean to listen." The corners of her lips twitched as if fighting a smile. "But that was great. You don't know how many times I wanted to tell that woman off, but in my position-"

"Makenna," he said, cutting her off, "can you take me to see my parents?" He wasn't mad at Makenna, but frustration raged through him.

Her smile faltered as she shifted back into her profession. "Right. Of course. I'll take you right away."

"Makenna." He grabbed her arm as she stepped away from him. "I'm sorry. I didn't mean to snap at you. It's just been a long day, and I have no idea what that woman is going to write. I'd just like to spend some time with my parents before," he shrugged, "you know."

She offered a small smile. "I do, so let's get you home."

CHAPTER 5

*B*ubba stared at the single level house that belonged to his parents. He had only spent a few years in this house as they had moved to Woodville when he was in high school, but for a time, at least, it had been home. Now, it felt like someone else's life. He hadn't been in this house for nearly five years, and he'd had no contact with his family since then either. What would they say? Would they hate him? His nerves twisted and knotted in his stomach, creating the feeling of having swallowed a lead weight.

"Should I come in with you?" Makenna asked, touching his arm.

The gentle feel of her hand focused Bubba, and he nodded. "That would be nice. There are parts I can't explain, but will your family mind you being out so late?"

A look of regret passed briefly over Makenna's face. "No one is waiting up for me except my cat, Tabitha."

Bubba knew that feeling. He'd tried dating a few women when he'd first moved to Fire Beach, but he could never completely relax. A sense of guilt about the women who had been murdered still plagued him even though he knew it wasn't his fault. Still, they had been killed simply because they knew him. That was hard to get over. Plus, deep down inside, a part of him feared it would happen again if he found someone and opened up about his past. It had just been easier to keep a distance and pretend he didn't need the company or the companionship, even though he did.

Perhaps Makenna was the same way. She'd definitely been devoted and eager when he'd met her five years ago. Maybe she too dealt with the guilt of never catching the arsonist or maybe her job was her life. To make captain as quickly as she had meant she was dedicated to her work. Perhaps, there was no time for a man in her life. He didn't know why that thought pulled at his heart.

"Okay, let's do this then." With a final deep breath, Bubba opened his door and stepped out of the police cruiser.

Makenna fell into step beside him as they walked up

the concrete path to the front door. His finger was almost on the bell when Makenna's hand stilled his arm.

"Wait, Bubba, I should tell you that your "death" hit your parents hard. They've aged faster than they might have otherwise, I think." Her eyes brimmed with apologies. "I just thought you should be prepared."

Her words broke his heart, but Bubba had known the ruse would be hard on his parents. He was the oldest, their first born, and no parent should ever have to bury their child, no matter how old. He had argued about it with Makenna on the night of his escape.

"I think we need to pretend you were killed, and you need to leave town," Makenna said as she paced her living room.

Matt shot up from the couch and threw his hands in the air. "Are you kidding me? I have a life here. My family is here."

"That's exactly my point." She turned and closed the distance between them. "I thought you were the arsonist because all the women were connected to you, but now I think you may have been the target all along. I think the arsonist was choosing women he thought you cared about, and when that didn't faze you, he targeted you. If we let him believe you're dead, then maybe this will end, but if he knows you're still alive, who will he target next? Felicity? Your mother? Your father? Do you really want their lives on your head?"

Matt stared into her eyes. Of course he didn't want to see his parents hurt or his foster sister, but was this really the only way?

"You really think the killings will stop if he thinks I'm dead?" She was asking him to give up everything - his life, his family, his job. Everything he had worked so hard for, but if it meant the killings stopped, he had to do it, didn't he?

"I don't know, but my gut says yes. Look, let's get you out of town and continue the charade. If the killings continue, I'll bring you back and explain to your family. But if they don't continue, if they end-"

"Then you'll know it was about hurting me all along," Bubba finished. Why anyone would want to hurt him was beyond comprehension. He was a fireman. He saved lives. He attended church and volunteered. He donated to charities. Why would anyone want to hurt him? He searched his memory for any altercation, any event that might have been misconstrued enough to set someone off, but he came up with nothing.

"I'm sorry, Matt. I know this is a lot to ask, but I think it's the only way."

And she'd been right. The killings had stopped. For five years. For five years, the people of Woodville had been safe. His family had been safe. But now that safety was crumbling yet again, and every bone in his body wanted to catch this guy. To stop him. To make him pay for the five years he had stolen from him.

He took a deep breath and then pressed the bell. The familiar melody echoed through the house, and a moment later, a soft shuffling sound carried forth. The lock clicked followed by a creak as the door opened, and then Bubba saw his mother's face for the first time in five years.

She did appear older. New lines had sprouted near her eyes and across her forehead, and her hair - once streaked with gray - was now completely devoid of color. But her eyes were the same deep pools of chocolate that he'd grown up seeing - the ones that oozed concern with every skinned knee and exuded love every time she kissed his forehead. They were filled with a resigned sadness now, but the light he remembered emerged as she recognized his face.

"Matt?" One hand flew to her mouth as the other gripped the door more tightly to keep her steady.

"Hi, Mom," he said, hoping she wouldn't pass out. He wasn't sure he'd make it through the door in time to catch her.

"Matt?" She let go of the door and then her hands were on his chest, his arms, his face, patting him as if to make sure he was real and not an apparition. "It's really you?"

"It's really me, Mom." Emotion choked his voice and tears stung his eyes, but it didn't matter. His mother threw her arms around him, and he returned the hug, relishing the warmth of family for the first time in half a decade.

"Margaret, who is it?" His father's voice carried in from the living room, and the familiar tone sent a flood of memories washing over Bubba.

"You better come see for yourself." His mother's voice was quiet, but it held a note of authority and moments later, his father appeared in the doorway. He too had aged, but the effects were not quite as dramatic. His hair was grayer, but he still stood straight and displayed the confidence in his posture that the military had taught him so long ago.

"Hi, Dad." His mother still clung to him, but he stood taller than she did and could see over her head.

"Matt? Is that you?" His father's eyes roamed his face as if he couldn't believe it, and then they turned to Makenna. "What is this? Is this your idea of some sick game?"

Bubba flinched at the sharp edge in his father's voice.

"If you'll let us come inside, I'll explain everything," Makenna said beside him. Though her exterior appeared brave, Bubba could see that his father's words had shaken her normal stoic face. A slight tremble hovered in her voice.

"Let's let them in, Patrick," his mother said, and though she did not let go of Bubba entirely, she shifted so that her arm remained firmly around him, but she could see his father. His father hesitated, but then he stepped back, and Makenna and Bubba entered the living room.

Waves of nostalgia washed over him as he took in the faded couch and the well-worn recliner where his father always drank his morning coffee. A painting his brother had made in high school still sat over the couch, and even the color of the walls was the same. It was like time had stood still in this living room, and Bubba wondered if they might be able to pick up where they left off.

⚇

"*I*'m going to call Felicity and see if she wants to come over," Margaret said as she motioned everyone to sit down. "She'll be so happy. She's had a rough week, but this might be just the thing to cheer her up."

"What do you mean a rough week?" Makenna asked. Though it was rare for an arsonist to be a woman, she was counting no one out, and as the murders had just started, anyone who'd had anything upsetting in the last month was a suspect in her book.

"She and her boyfriend broke up. They'd been together for years. She's pretty torn up about it, but she'll be so glad to know you're not dead." For a moment, she paused as if afraid Bubba might disappear if she wasn't touching him, but then she pulled out her cell phone and dialed.

Makenna sized up her options as everyone sat down. Patrick sat on the couch and Bubba took the recliner which left standing or sitting in the other chair. She didn't want to stay long and interrupt their family reunion, but standing seemed rude.

"Felicity, Matt is alive. He's here right now. You must come over and see him." She paused while she listened to the voice on the other end, and then her smile faltered. "But can't that wait until later?"

Makenna watched Margaret's reaction. Had his sister really declined coming to see the brother she thought was dead? That seemed odd to her. Had it been her brother, she would have dropped everything to come see him.

"Okay, I'll tell him. See you later." Margaret hung up the phone and stared at it a moment. "Um, she said she had some work she couldn't leave tonight, but she'll come see you tomorrow, Matt."

He flashed her a sympathetic smile. "It's fine, Mom."

She nodded, but she didn't appear convinced. "I'll call Jacob and Rachel. I know they don't live here anymore, but they'll want to know."

Bubba stood and placed a hand on her shoulder. "Mom, why don't you let Makenna explain first and then we can call anyone you want, okay?"

She nodded and allowed herself to be led to the couch. Bubba squeezed her shoulder and then returned to the recliner.

Makenna took a deep breath as she stared at Patrick and Margaret staring back at her. Flashbacks of the night she had come to tell them Matt was dead filled her mind, and she had to blink to dispel them.

"Five years ago, I sat here and told you that Matt had been killed in a house fire," she began, "but that wasn't the truth."

"You lied to us?" Patrick exploded, jumping up from the couch. "I'll have your badge for this."

"Please, Dad, hear her out." Bubba motioned for his father to sit back down.

She shot him a grateful look and then continued. "When the fires first started, the only clues we had pointed to Matt being involved. He knew all the women, and he had knowledge of how to start fires. But, then the killer went after Matt. He escaped that night and came to me. I realized then that Matt might have been the target all along. The killer chose the women he did in order to hurt Matt, and when that wasn't working, he went after Matt himself. I asked Matt to continue the charade that he had died. I knew that if the killings stopped, my assumption would be right. It meant Matt would have to stay "dead" to all of us, but it would keep you safe. If the killings had continued, I would have told you his death was a lie, and he could have returned home."

"I hated not being able to say goodbye," Bubba said, "but if it meant keeping you both safe, it was worth it."

A tear escaped Margaret's face, and she crossed the room to where Bubba was sitting. "Oh, my baby! That must have been so hard on you."

Makenna looked away from the touching scene. This was her fault. Her decision had torn this family apart five years ago, and those were years they would never get back. She'd have to live with the consequences of that decision for the rest of her life.

"I assume you've brought him back because of the recent murder." Patrick said from the couch. His crossed arms and passive face hid his emotions, and Makenna wondered what he was thinking.

"Yes, sir. The other night, a man was killed in a house fire. I believe it is the same guy even though we aren't sure why he is attacking men now instead of women. My hope is that when the killer finds out he didn't kill Matt after all that he'll mess up and give us some clue."

"So, you're using my son as a pawn once again."

"Dad," Bubba cut in, "she's not using me. She asked and I agreed. Besides, it allowed me to see you guys again."

"I don't like it," his father said. "She was wrong the

first time. What if she's wrong this time too, but you really do get hurt?"

"Dad, you know I can't just sit around knowing people are being killed. I have to at least try to help."

"You always were like that," Margaret said, stroking Bubba's hair. "I remember you used to always bring home stray animals to save them. Do you remember that?"

"I do, Mother."

Bubba appeared embarrassed by the hint of his childhood, and Makenna took that as her cue to let them catch up. "Well, it's getting late, and I have a feeling you'd all like to catch up." She turned to Bubba. "How about I swing by around nine in the morning and pick you up? I'd like you to go with me to interview some of the friends and employees of our victim."

"That sounds great. I'll see you then, Captain Drake."

Makenna stood and walked through the uncomfortable fog that filled the room. She might have reunited the family, but she'd also been the one who tore them apart. Nothing could change that, and she knew it would be a choice that would haunt her forever.

Was this why she had avoided having a family of her own? Was she so jaded from watching families grieve that she unconsciously pushed men away? Or was it simply her job? Even though they didn't have a lot of crime, her work load had increased dramatically with each promotion, and now as captain, she spent most of her time at work. Yes, that was probably it. There was no time for a family or even a man in her life as long as she stayed in her current position which left the question, was it time for a change?

CHAPTER 6

*M*akenna showed up at nine a.m. on the dot the next morning, and though Bubba wasn't sure what help he would be able to provide, he was glad for the excuse to get out of the house for a few hours. He loved his parents, and he loved catching up with them, but the emotional intensity had been a little much for him to handle. He hadn't been that close to anyone in the last five years.

"You ready?" Makenna asked him as he slid into the passenger seat of her cruiser.

"As I'll ever be, I guess."

"How was the reunion?" Her eyes glanced his way for only a moment, but he could tell his answer was important to her. He couldn't imagine the weight she must be carrying.

"It was good. I'd almost forgotten how much I missed having a family. I think I spent half the time just staring at them to prove to myself it was real."

Her jaw tightened, and he knew he had just made her feel worse even though that wasn't his intention. "Makenna, I don't blame you. You did what you thought was right." His words probably wouldn't relieve the guilt she was placing on herself, but he had to try.

"Thank you, Bubba, but I can't get back the time you lost, and that's a little hard to come to grips with."

There was nothing he could say at this point to change her mind, so he decided to change the subject instead. "Where are we going?"

"First stop is coffee and then we'll hit Peter's repair shop."

"Sounds good." Bubba stared out the window as Makenna drove through town. Not much had changed. The post office looked the same, and the parking lot still held the flagpole where the faded American flag waved gently in the breeze. Bubba was glad to see it still flying - there had been a debate over whether to take it down shortly before he'd left town. Evidently some new residents found it offensive, something Bubba would never understand.

A frozen yogurt store with a large neon sign was new as was some sort of gaming center. At least that's what he assumed it was from the name Creative Consoles.

And then there were the new hotels. He had never understood why the town had so many hotels. They had no claim to fame - no big sports team, no prestigious university, not even a famous statue like some of the towns near them. So, what brought people to Woodville? Was it the feeling of peace and tranquility the surrounding woods provided? Was it its location away from big cities? Was it the promise of a simpler life that the downtown buildings seemed to boast with their faded paint and weathered signage?

The coffee shop she pulled into was not the same one Bubba had frequented when he lived here as they were on the other side of town from the firehouse, but it was bustling nonetheless. He could remember a time when there was only one coffee shop in town, and it was never busy. Now, patrons filled every table, and a line of at least five more stood waiting to order.

"Busy place," Bubba remarked as he took in the interior which appeared much like most other coffee shops he had been in. The walls were a soft tan color which was brought out in the tile flooring. Tables capable of sitting four filled the room with a few smaller tables made for two by the windows, and one small couch sat nestled in the corner surrounded by a reading lamp and a glass table. A man immersed in his laptop took up most of the couch, and his books filled the other side. He lifted his mug to sip every few seconds but never seemed to look away from his screen.

"I know," Makenna said with a frown as she checked her watch, "but it's the best coffee in town, I think, so it's worth the wait."

The line moved quickly, and they reached the front in under ten minutes. "Welcome to Love a Latte," the employee said as she placed the previous payment in the register. "How can I-" Her words cut off as she raised her eyes and met Bubba's gaze. The color drained from her face as if she'd seen a ghost, which in his case, he guessed she sort of had. "Oh mylanta, as I live and breathe. Matt Fisher, is that you?"

"It is," Bubba said quietly, hoping she would do the same, but he should have known better. Daphne Rodgers had been a cheerleader and a prominent thespian in high school. Two things that rarely seemed to go together, but worked for Daphne. Outgoing and bubbly, temerity was not her strong suit.

"I thought you were dead. Everyone said you died in the house fire five years ago."

Heads turned their direction as her words floated over the hum of conversation. "Matt Fisher? I thought he died." "Who's Matt Fisher?"

Bubba felt the eyes of the customers on his back, and he turned and offered a small smile and a wave. Most simply stared at him in confusion, but one pair of eyes seemed to burn with an angry intensity. He stared back at the woman, curious as to why she might have so much hatred toward him, but he didn't recognize her. At least he didn't think he did. Perhaps, she was just angry that his entrance had disintegrated her silence. The laptop in front of her might hold her work as it did for the man on the couch or a book.

"It's a long story," Makenna spoke up beside him. "Can we just get our coffees to go?" Her authoritative voice dragged his attention back to Daphne who still stared at him with wide, disbelieving eyes.

"Sure. Sorry, I didn't mean to blow your cover. I'm just so glad to know you're not dead." She gazed at Bubba a little longer than necessary before taking their orders and payment.

Bubba still felt as if every eye was on him and every whisper discussed him as they waited at the end of the counter for the drinks. "It's going to be like this everywhere, isn't it?"

"It's what I was hoping for honestly," Makenna whispered back. "Word will spread like wildfire, and hopefully the killer will tip his hand."

"And if he doesn't?"

Makenna's lips pinched together, and she shook her head. Evidently she didn't want to think about that possibility either. They stood in silence for a minute, until their drinks were placed on the counter. Then, drinks in hand, they made their way out of the shop.

Bubba sighed with relief as he slid into the passenger seat. He was not used to being the focus of attention, and it would only get worse when Natasha's article came out.

"So, how do you know Daphne Rodgers?" Makenna asked as she pulled her door shut, closing the two of them off from prying eyes and ears. "She seemed mighty interested in you."

He took a sip of his coffee as he debated his answer. It was good; the hazelnut just strong enough to add flavor. "We went to high school together. She was the head cheerleader, and I was the captain of the football team, so everyone expected us to be together. I think she wanted to date me, but I was looking for a woman with a little more substance to her."

Daphne had been pretty with her auburn hair and bright green eyes, and she certainly was adored by everyone at the school, but Bubba had tried having a few conversations with her, and every time he had left feeling as if a few intelligence points had trickled out of his brain. So, he'd never been able to date her.

"Vapid?" Makenna asked as she pulled out of the parking lot.

Bubba smiled at her. "To say the least. She hounded

me all through school, and she would try to stop by the firehouse when she knew I was working."

"Do you think she felt slighted by you?"

"Enough to kill people?" Bubba couldn't believe they were having this conversation about Daphne Rodgers of all people. She hadn't even dissected the frog in biology because of her aversion to blood and all things disgusting - her exact words if he remembered correctly.

Makenna shrugged and, after sipping her own coffee, placed it in the middle cup holder. "Sometimes the visage we see is not the real person underneath."

"Visage? I don't think I've heard that word since high school English class."

A soft pink colored Makenna's cheeks, and she averted her gaze from his as she inserted the key into the ignition. "I may be guilty of reading a few classic novels in my free time."

Bubba chuckled. He was guilty of the same thing. At the firehouse, he hid his books under the mattress so as not to get razzed by Luca. He'd seen Bubba reading *A Tale of Two Cities* once and teased him mercilessly for the next week. "I'm guilty too, but I think you're wrong about Daphne. What you see is pretty much what you get, and I can't imagine her starting fires."

"You're probably right." Makenna sighed. "I'm just so focused on finding this guy that I'm seeing connections where there might be nothing."

"We'll find him." But as Bubba leaned back in the seat, he wasn't sure if he was trying to reassure Makenna or himself more.

❀

"*W*as this always here?" Bubba asked as they pulled into Peter's repair shop. "I don't remember an auto repair shop here before."

Makenna turned off the engine and stared out the windshield at the large black tire atop a metal pole that sat to the right of the building. Above the door, the sign read: Peter's Parts. "No, you wouldn't. It used to be a butcher shop until Peter converted it a few years ago. Seemed like a nice enough guy. A little rough on the exterior but good at his job."

"So, what are you hoping to find here?"

She turned to face him and shrugged. "I honestly don't know. A disgruntled employee, a jealous ex, a secret smuggling operation. Some reason for someone to want him dead." One corner of her mouth twitched up into a half smile. "I'm reaching at this point, but what have I got to lose?"

"I'll follow your lead then," Bubba said and then opened his door.

Makenna was actually a little surprised to see the open sign on the door. It was a small business, and she only knew of one other employee besides Peter. Was he trying to run it on his own? She supposed there could have been more than just the one guy she knew of. She'd only been here a couple of times when the check engine light came on in her cruiser. Though usually nothing, she could never ignore warning signs in her official vehicle like she could in her own car. They always had to be in perfect working order. Just in case.

The soft tinkling of an overhead bell announced their entrance, and a blonde popped up from behind the counter. Sparkly was the best word Makenna could come up with to describe her. Her tightly curled hair - most likely from a perm - fell to her shoulders. Glittery eyeshadow covered her lids, and her mouth glistened with some shade of pink. In addition, her top sported sequins that caught the light and appeared to shimmer. She looked anachronistic, like she belonged on a bad eighties sitcom instead of current time. Makenna had heard of previous fashions coming back in style, but even if that was the case, and she certainly hoped it wasn't, this was quite the odd outfit choice for someone working in a repair shop.

"Who are you?" Makenna asked. She'd never seen this woman before. She rarely forgot faces, and this getup was one that would regrettably be burned into her retinas for some time.

The girl placed her hands akimbo on her hips, and

Makenna expected her to smack gum loudly in her mouth as she spoke. "I'm Skye. Who are you?"

No gum, but the effect was still there. "I'm Captain Makenna Drake. Do you work here, Skye?"

"Do I look like I work here?" she asked rolling her eyes. "No. I'm Peter's ex-girlfriend. He owed me money, and I came to collect what I was owed."

"You can't steal money from his shop." Makenna hoped she wasn't going to have to arrest this woman and book her for theft. That hadn't been on her plans for the day and would mean paperwork to fill out, sucking her time from the more important matter at hand of finding a killer.

"I'm not stealing. I'm taking what's mine. He owed me a hundred dollars." She raised one manicured hand to flick her blond hair off her shoulder.

Makenna's eyes narrowed as her intuition perked into gear. As the saying went, money was the root of all evil, and she'd seen men killed for less. An ex-girlfriend with a monetary vendetta certainly had motive, and Skye had just made herself a suspect. "What for?"

"For spilling beer on my purse. I had to throw it away because I couldn't get the smell out," she wrinkled her nose and shivered, "but he promised he'd buy me a new one. Course then I saw him schmoozing with my ex-best friend a few days later. That's when we broke up, but he still owes me the money for the purse he ruined."

Makenna's head spun, and she glanced at Bubba to see if he found this as preposterous as she did. He shrugged and shook his head, clearly agreeing with her unspoken question. Did this woman have any idea how much motive she had just laid out before Makenna? Somehow, she doubted it. "Let me get this straight. Your boyfriend ruined your purse and cheated on you with your best friend?"

Skye's eyes widened as she nodded. "See? You get it. He wasn't a great boyfriend anyway, but cheaters get what they deserve."

"Uh huh. Skye, where were you two nights ago?" Makenna asked. This woman hardly looked capable of killing a spider should it run across her path, let alone a man, but not only did she have motive, she had also just stated that Peter had gotten what he deserved. Makenna would be remiss if she didn't at least ask.

"You mean when Peter was killed?" Skye's tone stayed completely even as if the thought of his death didn't affect her at all. "I was with Nick. Nick, come here and tell this fine police officer about our second date."

Nick stepped out of the work bay area, a complete opposite of Skye. As he was covered in grease and at least one tattoo that Makenna could see peeking from his collar, she assumed the bulging muscles protruding from his sleeves was what attracted Skye to him.

"You're dating Peter's employee?" Makenna asked. Now, she suddenly had two suspects. "Did Peter know?"

"He saw us together the night before he was killed," Skye said with a shrug as if this sort of thing happened every day. "Made a big scene about it and everything. I don't know why since he was still with my ex-best friend."

Makenna felt like slapping her forehead or pinching herself to make sure this was real. This situation was more like a "B" horror movie than actual life. "I'm afraid I'm going to have to bring you both in for questioning."

"What for?" Skye's wide eyes appeared clueless. Did she really not understand what she had just admitted?

"For saying too much," Nick hissed under his breath. Clearly he was the brains in the relationship which Makenna wasn't sure was saying much. "You just made us both suspects in Peter's death."

"What? But we didn't kill Peter. I can't be arrested. I can't have mug shots."

"I'm not arresting you." Makenna couldn't believe this woman was more worried about mug shots than a possible murder rap. "Not yet. But I do need to ask you a few questions. If you come with me, I won't have to pull out the handcuffs."

"I'll answer whatever you need as long as there are no mugshots."

"I can't believe you got me into this," Nick grumbled as he glared at Skye. "Now, I have to close the shop and lose money."

Makenna rolled her eyes at Bubba as she opened the back door for Nick and Skye. She'd quit her job on the spot if either of these two turned out to be the arsonist. Still, with so few leads, she couldn't let any possibility slip through her fingers.

"Looks like we'll be making a slight detour before talking to family. Do you mind?"

Bubba shrugged his broad shoulders. "I've got nothing else to do today."

Makenna flashed him a grateful smile. She felt taxed and overburdened by this case, but just having Bubba around calmed her a little though she didn't know why. Maybe it was the sheer masculinity he exuded. Maybe it was that he had been involved in the original case. Maybe it was the simple fact that she hadn't really conversed with a man not employed by her in ages, and it felt nice. She really needed to look into taking some time off when this case was wrapped up.

CHAPTER 7

*S*urprise shot through Bubba as they pulled up to the station and he noticed Felicity standing against the wall. His mother had said Felicity would try to see him today, but he had expected she would come to the house tonight, not show up at the police station. Though she hadn't appeared to change as much as his parents, the tight ponytail holding back her dark hair made her facial features appear more severe than normal.

Felicity was not his biological sister. After he and his siblings graduated high school, his parents felt the desire to help more kids, and they began fostering. Felicity was one of those foster kids. She joined their family when she was seventeen and Bubba was twenty-one, so he was not as close with her as he was with his biological brother and sister. But when Jacob and Rachel had moved away, he and Felicity had spent more time together, and they had grown closer the last year before he left.

Almost too close from Bubba's point of view though. There had been a few times when he'd heard her mumble snide remarks once or twice when he brought a woman home to meet his parents. As if she had any say. Still, she was family, and she'd had a rough childhood, so Bubba had always dismissed it.

"Why don't you take a few minutes to reconnect, and I'll come back for you when you're through?" Makenna asked as if reading his mind.

Bubba nodded and opened his door.

"Matt Fisher, I can't believe you let me think you were dead for five years."

He was unsure if the anger in her voice was real or forced, but before he could decide, she threw her arms around him in a giant hug.

"I've been so lonely without you here. How could you just leave without a word?" she asked when the hug ended and she stepped back.

"It was important to the case, Felicity. When the arsonist made an attack on me, Captain Drake figured we would all be safer if he thought I was dead."

A dark expression took over Felicity's face for a moment as she watched Makenna walk inside, and then as quickly as it came, it was gone. "Turns out she was wrong though, wasn't she? Since the murders have started again? So, you lost five years of your life and put us through the ringer for nothing."

Bubba didn't appreciate the tone in Felicity's voice even though that very thought had crossed his mind when Makenna first reappeared in his life. "She couldn't have known that though, and I was worried the killer would go after you or Mom and Dad. Plus, they didn't start again for five years, so for awhile, at least, Makenna was right."

"Hmph. Well, anyway, it's good to see you again, big brother." She placed a hand on his arm and squeezed. "I've missed you."

The last three words felt wrong as they landed on Bubba's ears, and his body stiffened. He didn't even know why, but something in the tone of them had been off. Perhaps he was making too much out of it though. Coming back to a town where everyone believed you were dead and stared and whispered about you was much harder than it had sounded initially, and it could be that he was the one off. He was definitely out of his comfort zone.

"It's good to see you again too, Felicity." He patted her hand before removing it from his arm. "You couldn't have missed me that much though since you didn't come over last night."

Another cloud crossed her face for a moment and

NEVER FORGET THE PAST | 69

then she smiled. "Yeah, sorry, I wasn't feeling well, and I had some work to catch up on, but you should come over for dinner tonight. Now that Roger and I are no longer together, I suddenly have a lot of free time on my hands."

The idea of a dinner alone with Felicity sent the hairs on the back of Bubba's neck up, but it would be rude not to accept, especially since she was family. "Sure, that sounds good. I'm staying with Mom and Dad, so maybe we should all do dinner together there."

Her lips pulled into a tight smile. "Yeah, that would be great. I'll see you tonight."

The door behind him opened as Felicity walked away. "Everything okay?" Makenna asked.

He watched his sister walk away and tried to put a finger on what was bothering him, but it was still too ambiguous. "Yeah, fine, it's just weird being back here. Everyone feels different or maybe I'm just different."

She placed a hand on his arm, and Bubba's gaze dropped to the heat creeping up his arm from her touch. How different her touch felt from Felicity's "I know it's hard, but it will get easier."

"I certainly hope so," he said as he followed her toward the station door, but as he grasped the handle, he wondered if that was true. Did one really ever get used to being the focus of town gossip? As the door swung open, a movement to the right caught his eye. He peered closer, but nothing appeared different.

"You okay?" Makenna asked.

"Yeah, I thought I saw something, but I must just be tired. I'm good." Still, he gave the surrounding area one more perusal before he followed Makenna inside.

🍥

"*J* can't take you in the interrogation room, but you can watch the whole thing from here," Makenna said, showing Bubba into a small room with a few chairs. On either side were large windows that looked into the interrogation rooms. Skye sat in the room on the left and Nick in the room on the right. She hadn't had many people watch interrogations, but the thought of Bubba on the other side of the glass sent her nerves coiling in her stomach. Was she afraid of messing up in front of him? Afraid of what he might think?

She shouldn't care what he thought. He lived in Fire Beach and her life was here. Besides, their schedules would probably never work, but she couldn't deny that there was something about Bubba. Growing up with two older brothers and learning to shoot rifles at the age of twelve, Makenna was used to defending and taking care of herself. She'd always felt tough and maybe a little too masculine, but Bubba made her feel feminine again. His six foot two frame dwarfed her five feet seven inches, and he exuded a protective vibe. She could imagine a life with someone like him, a life where she didn't feel like she always had to be the one calling the shots.

"I'm going to talk to Skye first and then Nick, though I doubt I'll get much," Makenna said, forcing her mind away from thoughts of curling up on a couch in Bubba's arms and to the task at hand. She turned up the knob to Skye's room. "This way you can hear us. When the interview is over, you can turn this down and turn the one on the other side up."

"Sounds good. I've never been on this side before," Bubba said with a playful smile. "I bet I'll enjoy it more."

Makenna swallowed the sting of embarrassment. Now that she knew him better, she couldn't believe she had ever thought he could be a killer, but she'd been greener then and the evidence had pointed to him - what little they'd had. Still, as much as she wished she could erase that experience, it had made her a better cop. She didn't jump to conclusions as quickly, and she challenged herself to consider other options.

"I'm sure you will," she said as she exited the room. She grabbed the folder with the case files from a hanging compartment outside of Skye's room and then pushed open the door.

"Do I get to go home soon?" Skye asked as Makenna

entered the interrogation room. "I thought this was going to just be a few quick questions."

"I'll get you out as soon as I can," Makenna said pulling out the chair across from Skye and sitting down. Her eyes wandered to the two-way mirror, but she forced them back to the folder in her hand. "Now, tell me again where you were on the night of the sixteenth."

Skye sighed and rolled her eyes. "I told you. I was out with Nick."

"Right, your second date. Did he pick you up?"

"No way," Skye said with a shake of her head. "I don't let a guy know where I live until the fifth date. Have to make sure he's not crazy, you know?"

Makenna bit her lip to keep from laughing. This woman exemplified crazy but didn't seem to recognize it. "Okay, so where did you meet?"

"At Darby's over on Sixth Avenue. I wanted to go dancing, but he wanted dinner first, so we decided to meet up there." Skye ran her hand through her blond mane, fluffing the hair as she did.

"And what time was that?" Makenna asked as she made a note in the file.

"Seven. I remember because we were only able to get one drink before their happy hour ended at seven-thirty. Who ends a happy hour that early?"

"I don't know." Makenna didn't drink, so she had no answer to the question. She'd only ever tried alcohol once, and it had been disgusting enough to turn her off of it after that. She still remembered leaning against the tractor on a hot, sunny day and watching her father pop the beer can open. The sound of the fizz had fascinated her, and she'd asked him for a drink. He'd paused and then, evidently deciding it wouldn't hurt, he'd held the can out to her. The smell had hit her first, that weird yeasty odor, but being the fearless child she was, she had tipped back the can and filled her mouth only to spit most of it out again when it hit her taste buds. That had been her first and last drink, so she had no idea what restaurants even had happy hours. "What time did you leave?"

"Eight thirty. I wanted to get into The Hop before they raised the price at nine."

The Hop was the closest thing to a club that Woodville offered. A couple had purchased the old warehouse a few years ago and fixed it up. Makenna had broken up many fights in that place.

"And how long were you two there?"

Skye placed her hands on the table and leaned forward. "Only till midnight. I had to work the next morning, and if I don't get a full eight hours, this is a puffy mess the next day." She made a circle around her face.

Midnight would be cutting it close. The fire was reported at one a.m., so she supposed Skye could have had time to get home, grab supplies, and get over to Peter's house, but every bone in Makenna's body was telling her that this woman was not a killer. "I'm assuming you left The Hop alone?"

"No, I left with Nick. We had taken one car from Darby's, so he drove me back there, but I left Darby's alone and so did Nick. Are we done now? I really have to get my nail fixed." She held out her hand and wiggled her ring finger. That nail didn't look any different than the others to Makenna, but she didn't say that.

"Almost. I have a few more questions, and I need to talk to Nick, but then I'll get you processed." Unless Skye said something revealing with the next few questions, Makennna didn't have enough to hold her even if she wanted to.

"Do you know any of these women?" Makenna pulled the photos of the three women out of the folder and spread them on the table.

"Her," Skye said, pointing to the fitness instructor. "I took a few classes with her, but I don't know the rest."

"Okay, thank you, Skye. I'll be back in a minute." Makenna slid the photos back into the folder and exited the room. She had to question Nick, but she was certain his answers would be the same.

CHAPTER 8

*B*ubba found the whole interrogation process fascinating, but a part of him felt they were wasting time interviewing these two. Skye had seemed to have nothing more than a weak motive to kill Peter, and if her alibi checked out, there would be no need to question her further. Plus, she didn't seem to know any of the other victims. Which begged the question of who would? Even though Woodville was a smaller town, what sort of person would know all five people from very different jobs and social statuses?

He turned the knob up on Nick's room, but before Makenna began the process, his phone rang. Cassidy's number flashed across the screen, and Bubba smiled as he clicked the talk button. It had only been two days, but he missed his friends back home.

"Hey, Cassidy, how are you?"

"I'm fine, Bubba. How are you doing there? Have you found any leads?"

"Not much yet. Makenna is interrogating a couple who knew the victim, but I don't think they did it." He glanced over at Nick and Makenna, but Nick leaned back in his chair, laid back and relaxed, as if he had nothing to hide.

"How's it been coming back from the dead?"

Bubba couldn't stop the sigh that escaped his lips. "That part has been harder for sure. You know me. I'm not one for the limelight, and it is on me everywhere I go here. How is everything back there?"

"Oh, you know, the same. A lot of sitting, a little bickering, and a few fires to put out. Thankfully, it's been a little quieter."

"Are Deacon and Luca still at it?"

Cassidy laughed on the other end. "When aren't they?"

"Yeah." Bubba missed the camaraderie of his friends. After he'd had to leave his family behind, Luca, Deacon, Cassidy, and the rest of the firefighters had become his surrogate family. As much as he was enjoying seeing his Mom and Dad again and even spending time with Makenna, he couldn't wait to get back. "Hopefully, we'll figure this out soon, and I'll be able to help you buffer them."

"We're all praying for you," Cassidy said.

Praying. That was something he hadn't done enough of since he arrived here. He should do that. If life had shown him anything, it was that he couldn't do much on his own, but with God, all things were possible.

"Thanks for the reminder, Cassidy. I need to do some more of that myself."

Before she could reply, he heard the sound of the alarm going off behind her. "Gotta run, Bubba, but we'll talk again soon."

The line went dead before he could say goodbye, but he took no offense to it. A fire took precedence over everything, and he'd been guilty of the same behavior more than once. He put the phone back in his pocket and decided now would be the perfect time to do what he should have done so much sooner.

"Lord, I'm not sure how to progress from here. Please give Makenna and me the knowledge on where to go and what to do next. And please keep the people of this town safe."

He let the words repeat in his mind as he turned his attention back to Nick and Makenna in the interrogation room.

*M*akenna thanked Nick and Skye for their time as she led them to the front door. "Please make sure you stay in town in case we have any more questions."

"We aren't going anywhere," Nick said. "I have a shop to run now at least until I find out if Peter left it to anyone else in his will."

Skye said nothing, but she nodded in agreement as she followed him out the front door.

"Well, that wasn't much of a help," Makenna said as she turned to Bubba. "Not that I expected it to be, but I was hoping we might gain some new knowledge."

"Maybe we will with his family?" Bubba asked.

"Yeah." Makenna checked her watch. It was nearly lunch time, but Kelsey had said Peter's parents were retired. Hopefully, they were the kind who stayed home and not the kind who filled their hours with traveling or shopping. "We better get going then."

As she reached for the door handle, the door flew open and Natasha Kingston entered, the glare on her face darker than a tornadic cloud. She shoved a paper at Bubba. "Here. I wrote your feel good resurrection story, but this isn't over yet. I'll be watching you, Matt Fisher." She narrowed her eyes at him before turning her vitriol on Makenna. "You too, Captain Drake. You better hope you find the killer this time or I'll strongly be advocating that we find a new captain." Before Makenna could utter a reply, Natasha spun around and left in the same whirlwind manner she had entered.

"Well, that's always fun," Makenna remarked, but Bubba's focus was on the paper in his hands. "Is it bad?" Natasha had stated it was a feel good piece, but Makenna knew that Natasha's definition of things wasn't always the same as her own.

"No, surprisingly, it's not, and it's probably exactly the publicity you were hoping for. I just hope it doesn't put my family in danger."

Makenna hadn't even considered how Matt's return might endanger his family, and she mentally kicked herself for not thinking it all the way through before acting. She'd thought she had gotten better at that but evidently not. She touched his arm and waited until he met her gaze. "We'll keep them safe, Bubba. I promise."

He nodded, but she knew he was thinking the same thing she was. How? They still had no idea who this killer was or how he chose his victims, and other than not sleeping at night, no way to stop him. But she was determined that she would not let his family be harmed any more than it already had been.

She led the way out of the station, and a few minutes later, they were on the road. Peter's parents' house was a small rambler on the outskirts of town that looked as if it had seen better days. Large curls of paint flaked from the house, and the grass appeared brown and crunchy. It hadn't rained much, so most people's grass was more brown than green, but this lawn was the epitome of neglect.

"I guess Peter didn't help out much around the house," Bubba said as his eyes scanned the yard.

"Yeah, it doesn't appear so." Makenna wondered how a son could do that. She didn't live near her parents, but if she did, she would definitely come help them out and she had little free time. Surely Peter had more time. She doubted he'd taken his work home with him like she did most days.

The porch creaked under their feet, and Makenna hoped it wouldn't crumble beneath their combined weight. There was no bell, so she rapped on the door and pulled out her badge. She'd worked with enough older people to know most of them wanted to see a badge before they would open their doors.

"Who is it?" a woman's voice called from the other side.

"Captain Makenna Drake with the police department," she said, holding her badge up to the peephole.

There was a moment of silence and then the door opened. A crack. Enough for a pair of eyes to peer out and observe them but not enough to see the woman's face. "Who's that with you?" The eyes flicked to Bubba.

"This is my friend Bubba. He's a firefighter who is helping me with a case. We need to ask you some questions about Peter."

The door opened a little farther to reveal a petite, weathered woman. Time had shown her little mercy. Age spots marred her face, and her hair while still brown was so thin in places that her scalp shown through. "I'm not sure what I can tell you. Peter stopped coming around about a year ago."

"Was there a reason?"

The woman shrugged and dropped her gaze to the floor. "He wanted money for his business. I guess it wasn't doing too well, but we didn't have any. We suggested he come work for his dad - he's an electrician - but Peter wanted nothing to do with that. Said if we didn't have money to help him, we weren't good parents. He never came over after that."

Makenna couldn't imagine someone disowning their parents simply because they couldn't afford to help, and she wondered if that was what had affected this woman so profoundly. "Was that his normal behavior?"

"No." His mother's eyes glistened with unshed tears. "He was the sweetest boy in high school. I don't know what made him change except maybe money. We never had much when he was growing up, but he always had food, clothes, and a roof over his head." She said this as if reassuring Makenna, or maybe herself, that she hadn't been a bad parent.

"When he first started his business, it was to help people. He'd always been good with cars - tinkered on ours from about the age of twelve - and he decided he would use that skill to help people. Lord knows we'd have been out more money than we could afford plenty of times if we hadn't had Peter to fix our cars, but then I guess he got greedy. Began raising his prices and complaining when people couldn't pay their bills."

Makenna's heart went out to the woman. She couldn't imagine how hard it would be to see your son behave so uncharacteristically and then cut you out of his life. "I'm so sorry for that and for your loss, but can I ask you just a few more questions?"

The woman sniffed, wiped a hand under her eyes, and nodded. "Sure, go ahead."

Makenna pulled the pictures out of the folder tucked under her arm. "Do you recognize any of these women? Ever see Peter with them or hear him talk about them?"

The woman took the photos and flipped them slowly. "No, I don't recognize any of them. Do you think they had something to do with his death?"

"I'm not sure, ma'am, but if I find out, I'll let you know."

"I know we hadn't spoken in a year, but I still loved

him." Her hand snaked out and grasped Makenna's arm. "Please tell me you'll find who killed my son."

"We'll do our best," Bubba said from behind her, speaking up for the first time.

"Thank you." The woman let go of Makenna and held Bubba's gaze for a moment before stepping back into the house and closing the door.

"We can't disappoint her, Makenna. She's lost so much already," Bubba said as they made their way back to the car.

Makenna knew that. She wanted to catch this guy as much as Bubba did. She wanted justice for the victims and families, and she didn't want any more lives lost, but the pressure was already high. She wasn't sure she could take much more.

CHAPTER 9

*S*he stared at the picture of Matt Fisher in the newspaper as the fire raged within her. How had he escaped? No one ever escaped.

Her mind raced back to the night she had started his fire. She had broken the window with her rock. Being a firefighter, Matt was too careful to leave his window open or unlocked even on a hot summer evening. She had poured the gasoline and struck the match. Just like she always did. And the house had caught fire. She had watched it burn herself. So, what had she missed? How had he gotten away?

She closed her eyes to picture the house in more detail and that's when she knew. She had watched the front of his house, expecting he would try and escape through the front door if he woke up, but he must have gone out his window. His bedroom had been on the opposite end of the house. How could she have been so careless? He was a fireman, trained to deal with fires. She should have had every exit covered, but how could she have? She was just one person. One angel on a mission.

So, what did she do now? Did she continue ridding the town of its blemishes or did she go after Matt Fisher and complete her mission from five years ago?

"You don't have to do either," a voice whispered in her ear. "You could stop now and leave this all behind. Find someone and settle down. Be happy."

"No, I can't," she yelled, shaking her head. "If I don't stop them, who will?"

No, she couldn't stop now. The face of the next victim flashed again in her mind. She'd been given a mission, and she would fulfill it. Then, she would go after Matt Fisher again.

She slipped on her gloves and grabbed the small gas can she always took. A pat of her pockets reassured her that her matches were still there, and she slipped out of her house and into the darkness.

She could have driven, but she enjoyed the feel of the night air. The moon guided her, granting her light from above, and the chill of the cool air honed her senses. She passed no one on her way which was not unusual. This town seemed to fall asleep as soon as the sun set. Stores closed by nine pm, and people shuttered themselves inside to watch their television shows or curl up with a book. No one seemed to suspect the evil that moved outside their windows.

All the lights were out in the house when she arrived. It was not a large house, but that simply meant he was squirreling his money away for now. She'd been told all about his scams and how much he was taking from innocent people, but after tonight that would no longer be an issue.

She walked the perimeter of the house, making sure to keep to the shadows. His neighbors weren't that close, but it wouldn't do to be seen.

No lights shone from inside the house, and she heard no noise either. Unfortunately, due to the chill in the air from the approaching fall, there also weren't any open windows. But that was okay. She had her rock.

Her hand found it in her pocket as she circled back to the living room window. These windows were her favorite. Partly because she didn't always know which rooms were bedrooms and in which bedroom the victim might be, but also because they almost always had curtains. And curtains loved fire.

When she reached the living room window, she scanned the area one more time to make sure no eyes were out, but it was silent. The night was her friend like always, and tonight, it shielded her. She withdrew the rock and smashed it against the window. Glass shards tinkled like tiny bells as they fell, and she held her breath to listen for any movement from within.

When there was nothing, she placed the rock back in her pocket and unscrewed the cap of the gas can. The spout fit perfectly in the hole, and she poured the contents in. Then she replaced the cap and set it on the ground beside her.

A tingle raced down her back as she pulled the book of matches from her other pocket. This was the part she waited for, the part that haunted her dreams until she fulfilled her mission. She struck the match and stared at the flame for a moment. Fire. Cleansing renewal. If only it could renew her, change her past, but perhaps that day was coming. Today was his day.

She dropped the match before it could burn her gloves and smiled as the flame caught the gasoline. A burst of heat flowed out of the window and then the greedy flames began their destruction. She picked up the gas can and stepped back. Now, she would wait. Wait until the black bag left the house and her mission was complete.

CHAPTER 10

*M*akenna slapped at her nightstand, trying to find the ringing phone in the dark. Her fingers touched the solid form and she brought it to her ear, clicking the call button as she did. "Captain Drake." Her voice sounded heavy with sleep.

"Sorry to wake you, Captain, but I thought you might want to know there's been another fire."

At the sound of the fire chief's deep voice, her eyes snapped open. "Another one? Are you sure?" She glanced at her watch. It was two a.m., but there would be no more sleep tonight.

"Yes Ma'am. I'm here now with my crew putting it out, but we were too late."

Makenna sighed as she flipped back the covers and stepped out of bed. "Another victim?"

"Afraid so. The address is listed as Dustin Cox."

"Okay, I'll grab my team and be there shortly. Can you try to keep the crowd back until we get there?"

"Already have a man on it."

"Thank you." She hung up the phone and changed into her uniform before she sent out the call to her team. It would be another long day for all of them.

Makenna was the first to arrive on the scene. Black smoke still wafted in the sky, but the flames had been doused. All that remained of the house was charred bricks and partial walls. She was getting tired of seeing this in her town.

The fire department had a spot light set up to see in the dark night, but she pulled her flashlight as she approached anyway. She didn't want to miss anything.

"Same as the last one?" she asked Chief Frye when she reached him. Frye had been the chief for ten years, so he'd been at all the previous fires as well.

He nodded and glared out at the scene. "Smashed window, gas, nothing left. It sure looks the same."

She understood his anger. They were supposed to be protecting the town, the citizens, but because she was failing, he was as well. "Thank you, Chief." She clicked her flashlight on and scanned the ground as she walked the perimeter of the house. Unfortunately, the hard ground didn't help. Her own steps left no prints, so she doubted the killer's had either.

"Hey, Captain," Tad said as he jogged up to her. Kelsey and Braydon were a few steps behind. "Any luck yet?"

"No, and I doubt we're going to find anything, but we gotta look. Kelsey, you and Braydon take a circle farther out. Scan for anything. Footprints, weapons, and don't forget to scan the crowd. This guy probably sticks around to watch. Maybe he's still here. Detain anyone who looks sketchy."

"You got it," Kelsey said as she and Brayden flicked on their own flashlights and began walking the perimeter she had assigned.

"I don't get it, Tad. How can this guy leave nothing? No prints, no weapon, nothing." Frustration colored her voice, but she couldn't help it. She had hoped bringing Matt back would disrupt the killer. Instead, she had another body on her hands and still nothing to go on.

*B*ubba woke to the sound of bacon sizzling and coffee dripping. He'd forgotten how noise carried in his parents' house. When he'd been in high school, he'd hated it. Not only could his mother hear his phone conversations no matter how quiet he was, but sneaking out, or in for that matter, had never been an option. Not that he was the type of kid who sneaked around, but he'd wanted the option. The one time he had tried though, his father had been there to meet him as he climbed in the window and nearly scared the daylights out of him. This morning though, he didn't mind. His stomach rumbled as he kicked back the covers and padded over to his suitcase to get dressed.

Across the room, his cell phone buzzed. It had to be Makenna. No one else he knew would text him at seven in the morning. He picked it up and sighed when he read the message. Another fire. Another life taken. Who was this guy?

"Good morning, Matt," his mother said as he entered the kitchen. "Did you sleep well?"

Matt. The name still caught him off guard, but he hadn't had the heart to ask his parents to call him Bubba. After all, he'd let them believe he was dead for five years. "I did, but unfortunately, Makenna will be here soon. There was another fire last night."

Fear clouded his mother's eyes as she set a plate of bacon and eggs in front of him. "Do you think it's safe for you here? Won't he go after you again?"

"I don't know, Mom. If I even had an idea of who this guy was, maybe I could tell you, but I've got nothing. Still, I can't go back to Fire Beach knowing this is happening. Now that I'm here, I have to stay until it's over." He speared an egg and shoved it into his mouth, but his mind wasn't on the taste. It was on his past life here. Who had he known who would want to kill him?

The answer was no one. He hadn't been mean to people in high school, and while there were women he hadn't dated, he had always been as nice as he could when turning them down. Then he'd gone to the fire academy and been a firefighter. His job was to help people. Had there been someone he saved who hadn't wanted to be saved? He'd heard stories about people like that going after the people who saved them, but no one had ever blamed him that he knew of.

The knock on the front door came just as he finished breakfast. "Gotta run, Mom. That will be Captain Drake."

"Please be safe," his mother said. "I don't want to lose you again."

"I promise." The words were easy to say, but he just hoped they were the truth.

"Sorry for the early text this morning," Makenna said as he opened the door. Dark circles ringed her eyes, and his heart went out to her. A part of him wanted to take her in his arms and ease her stress, and the other part of him wondered what he was thinking. He didn't have feelings for Makenna, did he? No, it was probably just seeing his family again and realizing his parents had something he might never have, but he couldn't deny there was something appealing about Makenna. She held herself with an air of confidence that he found attractive.

"It's no problem," he said shutting the front door behind him. "It's what I'm here for."

"Right," she said. Was that disappointment he heard in her voice? Was she feeling something too?

"So, what's the plan for today?"

"A quick stop at the station to gather information about our victim and then we'll go to his place of employment and interview friends and family just like yesterday."

"Sounds like a plan," Bubba said as he slid into the passenger seat and buckled the seat belt.

Ten minutes later, they were in the station and staring at another photo on the board. Another young man, probably in his late twenties. Bubba hated the loss of lives so young.

"This is Dustin Cox," Kelsey said. "Twenty-eight and single. He worked for Harrison Insurance where he was a claims agent. No family in town and no apparent connection to Peter, the first victim."

Makenna sighed. "Okay, Bubba and I will go to his job and see what we can find. You guys keep digging. There has to be some connection we're missing."

What were they missing? Two men from different backgrounds who worked different jobs. Why were they being targeted? Bubba shook his head in frustration sure that the answer was right in front of their faces.

CHAPTER 11

*M*akenna expected the stop at the insurance company to be routine, but as she parked the cruiser, a call came through on her radio from dispatch.

"Captain Drake, we have a report of a woman acting erratic in the Harrington Insurance building."

Makenna exchanged a startled glance with Bubba. "Harrington Insurance? Are you sure?"

"Yes, ma'am, the call just came in. Should I send Lieutenant Brewer or Officer Cook?"

"No need. I'm here at the building with Matt Fisher. We'll check it out." She clicked the radio off and glanced at Bubba again. Though he wasn't a cop, firefighters were also trained to deal with situations like this, and his hulking presence certainly wouldn't hurt in de-escalating the situation. "Feel up to this?"

"Whatever I can do."

Makenna nodded and opened her door. As she stepped out of the car, she could hear what sounded like screaming coming from inside the building. She shot Bubba a concerned glance as her hand touched the butt of her gun.

She led the way up the walkway and pulled the door open. A harried-looking receptionist glanced up at them and motioned them to continue. A glass door separated the reception area from the office area, but the screaming was audible even before Makenna opened the door.

"Where is it? I just want what he owed me." An edge of hysteria filled the shrill voice.

As Makenna opened the door, a blond woman came into view. She held a knife in her hand and was whirling around with it whenever anyone came too close to her.

"Ma'am, I need you to drop the knife," Makenna said as she stepped closer.

The woman turned wide, frantic eyes on her. "Not until I get what he owed me. They know where it is, but they won't tell me."

"Okay, so how about you tell me? Who owes you and what does he owe you?" Makenna scanned the area as she stepped closer to the woman. Most of the employees were cowering in fear but she never knew when one might decide to be a hero and send the situation careening downhill.

"Money. He owes me money. I filed a claim when my house was broken into a month ago, and he's been sitting on my claim. I need that money to fix my house." Her hand trembled sending the knife wavering like a shiny floating ripple.

"All right. I hear you. Why don't you put the knife down and tell me who your agent was?" Makenna held her hand out as she took another step closer to the woman. From the corner of her eye, she saw Bubba move off to her right, and she knew he was placing himself behind the woman.

"Dustin Cox was my agent, and I know he has my check somewhere in his desk, but they won't let me look." She pointed the knife at a balding man in a suit who Makenna deduced to be the boss. "I just want my money."

"Ma'am, I'm sorry you didn't get the money owed to you, but I'm here now. I'm Captain Makenna Drake, and I can get them to help you if you just put your knife down."

The woman's eyes twitched as if she wasn't sure she believed Makenna's words. But after a moment, her hand opened, and the knife clattered to the floor.

Makenna rushed in and snapped the cuffs on the woman.

"What are you doing?" the woman asked. "I thought you were going to help me."

"I am, but I also need to ask you a few questions, and I need to make sure you aren't going to harm anyone until I can do that, okay?" Makenna motioned Bubba to come forward and take the woman's arms. At the sight of him, the woman stopped struggling and dropped her eyes to the floor, but not before Makenna saw the sheen of unshed tears.

Makenna picked up the knife and turned to the balding man. "Is there truth to her words? Did Dustin Cox have her check?"

"I don't know," the man said. "I'll have to look into it, but I can tell you that Dustin was on our radar for insurance fraud. She's not the first one to claim that money owed was never received."

"Okay, I'm going to need you to investigate as quickly as you can, and then I want all the cases he was working on." Makenna felt her suspect pool growing. If this woman was angry enough to come in with a knife, could she have been angry enough to light his house on fire? Could any of his other victims?

The man nodded. "I'll compile them myself and send them over this afternoon."

"Great, thank you." She glanced over at the sniffling

woman who no longer appeared a threat to anyone. "Do you want to press charges?"

The man's lips pinched together for a moment. "Not if she's right. If it turns out Dustin was stealing her money, then let her go."

Makenna nodded and picked up the knife. She handed it, handle first, to Bubba as she took the woman's arm. "What's your name, Ma'am?"

The woman lifted a splotchy, tear-stained, and defeated face. "Chloe. I wasn't really going to hurt anyone. I just need the money."

"Okay, Chloe. I understand that, but brandishing a knife is not the best way to go about getting what you want. I'm going to take you to the station and ask you some questions, but we'll figure it all out."

Chloe nodded, but she said nothing more as Makenna led her out to the car. A sigh escaped Makenna's lips as she closed the door after securing Chloe in the back seat.

"Do you always see this much action?" Bubba asked with a teasing smile. He was obviously trying to ease the tension of the situation.

She smiled and shook her head. "No, it's usually pretty sleepy around here, but these murders have everyone acting crazy. And this admission just opens up a whole new bunch of suspects."

"Well, I don't know what I can do to help, but I'm

here. Whatever you need."

His last three words stirred something in Makenna's heart and she sneaked a glance at him. She knew he was talking about helping with the case, so why did it feel as if some other innuendo existed in those words?

As he held her gaze, she felt something between them shift. She cleared her throat and tore her eyes away from his penetrating stare. "Thank you. I'll question her if you want to grab some lunch and then maybe we can begin looking into other victims of Dustin Cox's."

"I'd be happy to. Would you like me to pick up something for you?"

"A sandwich would be great," she said as her stomach rumbled at the thought.

"You got it." The smile he sent her direction caused her heart to skip a beat, and she shook her head to bring it out of the clouds and back to the case at hand. She could daydream later when her town was safe again.

$\mathcal{B}$ubba opened the door to Charlie's, the small family run sandwich shop just a few blocks from the police station. Charlie's had been one of his go to restaurants when he had worked at the fire station, and he was glad to see they were still in business.

The traditional lunch crowd packed the interior, and Bubba scanned the area as he waited. He wished they had more information on the arsonist. With so much ambiguity, he couldn't help wondering if anyone in this room could be the suspect. Would he know it if he spoke to them? Would the killer give off some creepy vibe or feel?

"Can I help you?"

Bubba glanced up and realized the line had moved without him and the cashier was waiting for him to order. He didn't recognize the woman, and he wondered if Charlie and Darla still owned the place. They had been the sweetest couple always making time to circle the room and ask about the food or life in general. Charlie would sometimes even pull out a chair and sit with patrons until Darla good-naturedly ushered him back to work. He would hate to hear they no longer ran the place.

Stepping up, he placed his order and handed over the money. She took it and handed him a receipt as if it were the most normal thing in the world. He had almost forgotten that feeling. The stares and whispers as he passed had become so common that when they didn't happen, it felt odd.

When his name was called, he grabbed the food and made his way toward the front door, but before he reached it, a hand landed on his arm. He whirled to see who had touched him and found himself face to face with Daphne.

"Hey, Matt," she said in her soft, flirty voice. "I was hoping I would run into you again. I know we never got a chance in high school, but I thought maybe we could do dinner or lunch?"

Bubba forced his face to remain impassive, but the thought of having dinner with Daphne ranked about as high as watching paint dry in his book. He had a feeling it might be about as intellectually stimulating as well. "I don't know if I'll have time as I'm helping Captain Drake out, but if I do, I'll let you know."

Her smile faltered for a moment, and a cloud passed over her eyes, but then she brightened again. "Sure, sounds good. You know where to find me."

"That I do. Good to see you again, Daphne."

"You too. Be careful out there," she called to him as he opened the door.

He turned back to her, the choice of her words stopping him in his tracks, but she had already turned away and was stepping up to the counter. What had she meant by that? Did she know something about these murders? Or was that just something she said?

As quickly as it was gone, the unease returned, and Bubba returned to the prayer he'd uttered the day before. He hoped they found the killer soon. This constant state of uncertainty was wearing on him.

He opened the door and nearly collided with Davis Redman. Davis had been a fellow firefighter, but Bubba had never been close to him. There always appeared to be a current of anger brimming just under his surface.

"Well, if it isn't Matt Fisher back from the dead."

Bubba flinched slightly at the hatred that assaulted him with Davis's words. "Davis, good to see you again."

"Is it?" He folded his beefy arms across his chest and leaned back. "We had a funeral for you, you know? Dress uniforms and all. Your picture hangs on the wall with the other firefighters who actually lost their lives in a fire. Guess we can take that down now, huh?"

Bubba could feel his own temper rising. Normally cool headed, this guy was pushing all the right buttons. "Look, Davis, I didn't ask to be targeted, and if I hadn't thought my family was in danger, I wouldn't have left. I'm sure if you had been in my position, you would have done the same thing." Bubba had no idea if the man even had family or if he was close to them, but he had to assume there was decency in Davis somewhere even though something had clearly happened to make him fixate on the negative so much.

"That's where you're wrong." Davis leaned forward and for a moment, Bubba thought he was going to poke him in the chest. "I would have stayed and found the person responsible. Stopping them is the only real way to protect your family."

"Then I guess we'll have to agree to disagree, Davis." Bubba was careful to keep his voice even. Clearly, Davis was agitated at him, but getting in a fight was not something he wanted to do. He hadn't seen Natasha, the dogmatic reporter, today, but if she truly were watching his every move, the last thing he needed to do was hit anyone - even someone who might deserve it.

"Now, if you'll excuse me, I have to get back to the police station. Captain Drake and I are working hard to find the killer so that no one else has to go through what

I or my family did." Before Davis could say another word, Bubba stepped around him and continued to the police station. He couldn't help wondering if his other firefighter brothers felt the same way as Davis though. A part of him wanted to go to the firehouse and apologize and the other part of him felt that might just make the situation worse.

"I don't know why you brought me back here, Lord, but I sure hope something good comes out of it," Bubba said under his breath as he pulled open the door to the police station.

"Hey, you okay?" Makenna asked as he entered her office with the food.

"Yeah." He set the bag down on her desk. "I just had a run in with a guy from my past. He was pretty angry that I faked my death. I guess I never realized people might be mad; I just thought they would understand the reasoning."

She rose from her chair and crossed to the space in front of him. "Bubba, I wish I had the words to make everything better. I know that everything you are going through right now is my fault, and I just…" She shook her head as if her words had run out mid sentence. Her bottom lip folded under her top teeth, and for the first time since he'd known her, a sense of vulnerability floated around her.

He placed a hand on her arm and forced it to stay

there and not wander up to her dark hair which fell to her shoulders today. "It's no use living in the past, Makenna. We have to focus on today and finding the killer."

Her eyes met his, and every nerve in his body tingled. He wanted to kiss her, to take her in his arms and forget their current predicament for just a moment, but before he could, Natasha's voice carried across the room.

"Now this will make a great headline. Captain Drake fails to find the killer because she's too busy canoodling with the victim who got away." She lowered her iphone and flashed her predatory smile at them.

Bubba dropped his hand from Makenna's arm but not before he felt her tense.

"What are you doing here, Natasha?" Makenna's voice was cool but professional.

"I came to see if you had a comment about the most recent death but clearly you're too busy to be doing your actual job."

"That's enough," Bubba said. "Makenna has been working tirelessly to find this killer-"

"Bubba, please," Makenna said, cutting him off. She shot him a look that said she appreciated his help but could defend herself, at least in this situation. Then she turned back to Natasha. "I appreciate your doggedness on this case, Natasha, but you know I can't discuss details of the case with you. What you can tell your readers is that we are doing everything we can to catch this guy and that if the public wants to help, they can be vigilant watchers and report anything suspicious."

"Hmph, I'll be sure to do that, Captain Drake, but you should remember that a picture's worth a thousand words." She waved her phone as a reminder. "I'll see myself out."

"That woman is a piece of work," Bubba said when he was sure Natasha was gone.

"She is," Makenna said with a sigh, "but she's also right. Perception is everything, and I need to make sure that the town believes we are doing everything we can. The last thing I need is a vigilante on my hands trying to take matters into his own hands because he thinks we aren't doing enough."

"Of course," Bubba said, but he caught her unsaid words. They couldn't be seen in a compromised position like that again. Even though nothing had happened, they needed to be careful to keep their relationship strictly professional. "I take you had no luck then?"

Makenna ran a hand through her hair as she walked back to the other side of her desk. "None. She's clean. I don't know what I'm missing, Bubba."

"I don't either, but I know when I get stuck that praying often helps." He took her sandwich out and set it in front of her.

"You're a believer too?" she asked, looking up at him.

"I am. I think I always believed in God - my parents took us to church every Sunday - but I don't think I had a relationship with Him until I left here. When I ended up in Fire Beach and had to start over, that's when He really took ahold of me. How about you?"

"Kind of the same," she said as she unwrapped her sandwich. "I learned to lean on Him when I couldn't solve the case five years ago. Sometimes, He's all that keeps me going."

"You never wanted a family?" Bubba hoped he wasn't being too personal as he pulled up a chair and sat across from her.

"Never had time for one, I guess, but I think about it."

The look she gave him as she spoke sent his heart thumping in his chest. His brain understood they had agreed to remain professional, but he hadn't felt his heart move like this in a long time. Was he falling for Makenna?

*M*akenna stared at the information in the report and tried not to think about the almost kiss with Bubba. He had been about to kiss her.

She knew it, could see it in his eyes. And she'd wanted him to. At least until Natasha had shown up and ruined everything. She had a knack for that, but Makenna couldn't blame Natasha this time. She was asking what everyone else wanted to know. When was she going to find this killer and put a stop to him?

Besides, it wasn't Natasha's fault that Makenna was sitting here with a stomach full of conflicting emotions. No, that was completely her fault. She shouldn't have told Bubba they needed to stay strictly professional. They did, at least until this case was over, but now she was afraid he'd taken her words to mean she had no interest in him and that was about as far from the truth as one could get. Since she'd driven to Fire Beach to get him, her mind had warred between thoughts of the killer and thoughts of Bubba.

She had tried convincing herself that the thoughts of him were just feelings of remorse for his lost years, but she knew that wasn't true. Thoughts of remorse wouldn't have her imagining what his hands would feel like on her neck, in her hair. And they certainly wouldn't have her imagining what his lips might feel like pressed against her own. But she'd had to go and ruin it. Now, she had her feelings for him along with feelings of guilt for making him think she didn't care along with her feelings of failure at not catching the killer. To put it mildly, she was a hot mess.

She chanced a glance at him from the corner of her eye as she chewed on the sandwich he had brought her. She hadn't told him how much she enjoyed salami, so she was surprised he had returned with an Italian sandwich for her. He was definitely surprising. And dedicated. His eyes were focused on the paper in front of him as well. He'd offered to help her go through the list of Dustin's clients as they ate, and though she could have had Tad or Kelsey do it, she'd agreed. She enjoyed spending time with him, even if it was searching for a killer, and she knew she would miss it when he was gone.

Gone. She needed to keep reminding herself of that fact too. When this case ended, he would probably return to Fire Beach and then where would she be? Alone. Again.

Makenna hadn't meant to marry her work, but it had sort of happened. In the beginning, she had thrown herself into the job in order to learn and prove herself, but then the case five years ago had happened. When everyone else had left, she quickly climbed the ladder, and once she made captain, she rarely had time for anything else. Or anyone else.

Still, she couldn't deny the feelings. She hoped one day to find someone she could share evenings and weekends with, someone she could take to church, and someone who could listen when she needed to process cases. She could see Bubba filling that role in her life, but she knew that wasn't reality. When this case ended, he would return to his life, and her life would continue here.

"What?" he asked, catching her staring at him.

Heat filled her face. "Nothing, I was just thinking it's been nice having you here."

He smiled at her. "It's been nice being here with you. I'm certainly glad I'll get to be in my family's life again, and maybe..." he trailed off and looked away as if unsure how to finish that sentence.

"Maybe what?" she asked. Was he going to tell her she'd been wrong? That they could have a relationship and still solve this case?

"Maybe I'll come back more often and stop in and see you."

"I'd like that," she said, but that wasn't what she had been hoping to hear. She didn't know if a long-distance relationship would last, but she might be willing to try it with him.

"Hey, look at this," he said, pushing his paper her direction. "This looks like a lot of denied claims doesn't it?"

Makenna stared down at the paper, but she was no insurance agent. She had no idea if these were legitimate denials or Dustin's denials that he had then pocketed. It appeared they would need more information. "Yeah, it does. We should definitely look into that."

And the moment was gone. It was back to work. She

shouldn't be sad; this was the life she'd chosen, but she couldn't help wondering if maybe she had made the wrong choice. Her mind wandered back to the night she had sent Bubba away.

Makenna's eyes snapped open at the ringing of her phone. The clock beside her read two in the morning. Who would be calling her at two in the morning? There was only one answer to that question. Work. Snapping awake, she grabbed her phone and pressed the call button.

"Sergeant Drake here."

"Makenna, we've had another fire. I need you to get over to 232 Overside Street." The voice of her captain was firm, so even though she knew someone else had to be working the night shift, she didn't argue.

"232 Overside?" The address felt familiar in her head. "Wait! Isn't that Matt Fisher's address?" Matt Fisher was a local fireman, but he was also her number one suspect right now. He knew all of the previous victims, even if only slightly, and he understood fire. She just hadn't figured out a motive yet, but now her captain was telling her he was not the arsonist, but a victim.

"Yes, it is. Get over there and see if you can help determine if he set this fire himself to divert suspicion."

"Yes, sir. I'll be right there." She ended the call and grabbed her uniform. She had just holstered her gun when the pounding began on her front door.

She peeked through the spyhole surprised to see Matt Fisher standing on her front porch. He was clad only in shorts and a pair of tennis shoes, and he appeared out of breath.

"He got my house, Drake," he said when she opened the door. "Now, do you believe I'm not your suspect?"

For a moment she wasn't sure what to believe. Was this part of his elaborate plan? It seemed crazy, but then he would have to be crazy to be starting fires like this. However, when she looked in his eyes, something in her knew that he was innocent. She stepped back and opened the door for him. "Come inside and tell me what happened."

As he stepped past her, she scanned the area for anyone who might have followed him, but the neighborhood seemed to sleep on around them. She shut the door and turned to Matt.

What if instead of telling him to run that night she had worked with him then? Would they have ended up together? She didn't know, but the one thing she did know was that she couldn't live in the past. Those decisions were made and done. She could only move forward from here.

CHAPTER 13

*S*he approached the police station as she made her way home that evening. It was not her normal route, but some unseen force seemed to guide her in that direction. She wanted to see if Matt was still there. Matt, the man who should be dead. The one who had gotten away. The one she needed to take care of, but not yet. She'd been given another name, and he would have to come first.

As she reached the corner where the station sat, voices carried on the air. She flattened herself against the corner and peeked around. Matt and Captain Drake were talking as they walked to her car.

Their words were too soft to make out, but she could read the attraction between them. What did Makenna

Drake see in him? Didn't she know what he had done? A renewed anger washed through her.

"I should take him now," she whispered. She didn't have her gas can, but the matches were in her pocket. They were always in her pocket, a tactile device she could touch and draw comfort from when necessary. Would a car catch fire with just a match? She doubted it, and it would be stupid to attack them in front of the station. Someone was probably still inside, and if she were caught now, she couldn't finish her mission.

"His time will come." She felt the voice more than heard it, but it calmed her seething nerves nonetheless. The voice was never wrong. If it said Matt's time would come, then it would. And she would watch him take his last breath when it did. This time she would be sure.

An engine hummed to life, and a moment later, she watched the car drive away. She waited until the car turned the corner before she continued toward her house. She still had hours to kill. Hours before she could fulfill her mission and rid the town of one more monster.

The large house appeared before her, and she paused momentarily. What if he had an alarm system? He was wealthy enough to afford one. Not only was he the prominent doctor in town, but she had it on good authority that he was overcharging patients and pocketing the extra.

It almost always came down to money, didn't it? Money ate at men's hearts and fueled greed and jealousy. The gospels had been correct when they stated that it was "easier for a camel to pass through the eye of a needle than for a rich man to enter the kingdom of God." Just another reason, she had been called to rid the town of these men. They would never enter the kingdom of God, so there was no reason for them to continue life on Earth.

"Leave it alone," the voice whispered. "It's too dangerous."

"No," she hissed. She hated that voice. That weak voice. The weak voice had controlled her for too long. Until she had broken free five years ago. Until she had been shown what she had to do.

The first kill had been the hardest because the voice kept trying to dissuade her. She had hesitated when she struck the first match and burned her finger through her gloves, but she knew her mission had to be completed. Her first mission had been simple - to hurt Matt Fisher. He needed to pay, but he couldn't be first. He needed to feel the pain she had felt, so she'd been shown women in his life.

After Matt's death, the visions had stopped. She had missed them, but without them there was no sense of purpose, so she had let the weak voice take over again. Until the visions returned. But this time they had been different. They told her she had proved herself, that she had earned a more important mission - to rid the town of those who cheated and stole. And Dr. Hayworth was one of the worst.

She walked around the perimeter of the house looking for any signs of a security system but saw none. No cameras, no motion sensors, no lights of any kind shining from within. Probably too confident in the safety of this small town to spend the money. She returned to the living room window.

She tried lifting the window, but it was locked just like the one last night. She cursed the changing weather. Winter was coming, and the need for open windows had diminished. She withdrew the rock from her pocket. It was the perfect size really, small enough to fit in her hand but large enough to make the necessary hole in a window. She drew her hand back and slammed the rock into the side of the window nearest the curtain. Her body froze as the glass shattered, and she waited for any indication it had woken the occupant. But the silence pressed on.

Unscrewing the cap, she poured the contents of the gasoline into the window and then set the container on the ground to pull out the matches. The moon had disappeared behind a cloud offering the perfect shadow of obscurity. She struck the match, enjoying the heat and the light of the dancing flame for a moment before she dropped it inside the window. It only took an instant to find the gasoline, and then the blaze climbed to the roof.

She stepped back to admire her work, but suddenly a light flicked on in the house. She hissed under her breath and turned to run. There would be no sticking around to enjoy this one.

"I told you so," the voice whispered as she fled the scene. Too late she realized she had forgotten her gas can, but no matter, she always wore her gloves. There would be no fingerprints on it, and she could easily pick up another one. No, the focus now was getting away unseen. She was almost off his property when her foot slipped in a soft piece of ground, and she tumbled to the ground. Pain tore through her hand and she lifted it to see a jagged cut. She looked around for the rock she must have landed on, but the moon had slipped behind the clouds again. It was too dark.

"Run," the voice whispered again. "Get out now."

"Shut up," she hissed at the voice, but a trickle of fear pressed in on her. Had she left a footprint when she slipped? Had she bled on the rock? Surely, she was far enough away that it wouldn't matter. Would they search this far? She should stay and search, but then the faint sound of sirens in the distance reached her ears. Would they have been alerted so quickly? He must have called. That was the only explanation.

Two failed missions. The failure pressed down on her like a smothering blanket. She was losing her touch. No, it was Matt's fault. Seeing him alive again had thrown her for a loop. She would have to put this mission on hold and take care of him. Him and the female cop.

CHAPTER 14

"You look tired," Bubba said as he slid into the passenger seat of Makenna's cruiser. Dark red lines stood out in her bloodshot eyes, and the circles from yesterday were even darker.

"It was an interesting night last night." She put the car into reverse and backed out of the driveway. "There was another fire, but thankfully Dr. Hayworth was awake. He managed to call the fire department and get out before the fire reached his bedroom."

"Did he see anything?" Bubba asked.

"No, it was after midnight and dark. He said he would normally have been asleep, but a case was bothering him. We processed what we could last night, but it's hard to find evidence in the dark, so we're headed back out there this morning."

"Sounds good," Bubba said, but his eyes were on a woman across the street. It was the same woman from the coffee shop the other day. "Makenna, do you know her?" he asked, pointing at the woman.

Makenna followed his finger and nodded. "Yeah, that's Rachel Hanes. She's a bit of an odd duck but harmless. Keeps to herself mostly. Why?"

Rachel Hanes. Why did that name seem familiar to him? He could feel it, how he knew her, circling in his brain, but he couldn't place her yet. "I saw her at the coffee shop too, and she looked angry at the sight of me. Now, she's here near my parents' house. It just seems odd."

"Hmm." Makenna's eyes were back on the road. "She wanders the city a lot, but that is a little odd. We'll look into it when we get done this morning."

Bubba nodded and tried to dislodge the unease from his stomach. Could she be important? Was he missing something by not remembering who she was?

Fifteen minutes later, they pulled up to the charred house. Another police cruiser sat in the street and yellow crime scene tape surrounded the area.

"Stay close to me so you don't accidentally contaminate the scene," Makenna said as she parked the car.

Bubba fell into step beside her, but as he approached the charred house, visions of his own narrow escape filled his mind. He could hear the crackling flames and feel the heat seeping in through his bedroom door. He shook his head to clear the past and focused on the house in front of him.

Though Makenna had said the fire department arrived quickly, most of the house was still blackened and charred. The far end, which must have housed the bedroom the doctor escaped from, was still intact though Bubba knew smoke damage would have ruined the interior of it as well.

"Captain, I think you're going to want to see this," Tad called from the left.

Bubba followed Makenna to where Tad and Kelsey stood staring down at the ground. A yellow evidence flag stuck up out of the ground marking something.

"Is that a shoe print?" Makenna asked.

"It is. It's not clear because it looks like maybe the person slipped, but that's not the weird part."

Bubba stared down at the footprint trying to discern what Tad was talking about, but he didn't see anything out of the ordinary. It looked just like a-

"Is that a woman's shoe print?" Makenna asked.

And then Bubba realized. The print did look too thin and too short to belong to a man which meant that if this print did belong to the arsonist, they were looking not for a man, but for a woman.

"It sure looks that way to me, Captain."

"Well, this changes everything," Makenna said.

"There's more," Kelsey said and pointed to another flag sticking up a few feet away. "We found a rock with blood on it."

"Is it enough to process?" Makenna asked.

"I don't know, but we'll sure try. Regardless, if these belong to the arsonist, she'll probably have a cut somewhere on her. Judging by the distance, I'd say her hand or arm. Maybe even her face if she's shorter."

A woman. She had definitely not been expecting that. Female serial killers were rare. Female arsonists even rarer. "We need to go back and look at the last victims again. And Dr. Hayworth. I want everything on him you can find."

"What are you thinking?" Bubba asked as he followed her back to the car.

She stopped and faced him. "Statistically speaking, very few women kill, but those who do generally fall into two categories: killing for lust or visionaries. Since we have both male and female victims, that makes killing for lust less likely which means we are probably looking for a visionary."

"What's a visionary?" Bubba asked.

"Someone who kills because they think someone told them to or because they see it as getting rid of the scourge of society. Generally, visionaries have had a psychotic break which makes them harder to catch because they lead a normal life the rest of the time. If our killer is a visionary, she could be anyone."

"What would cause a psychotic break?"

"Abuse generally, especially in childhood. Breaks generally form early in life but lay dormant until something triggers them like a death or a-"

"A breakup?" Bubba asked, interrupting her.

"Maybe." She narrowed her eyes at him. Something was clearly on his mind. "Why? What are you thinking?"

"It's probably nothing." His words held a note of dismissal, but the nervous tell of his hand rubbing across his chin told her it might be something. "Felicity came over for dinner the other night, and she just seemed," he paused as if searching for the right word, "agitated. Plus, remember my mother said she broke up with her boyfriend shortly before the first recent murder. She said they had been together for years."

"Okay, but that's not much to go on," Makenna said, wondering where this accusal was coming from. Having been falsely accused himself, she couldn't imagine Bubba doing the same unless there was more he wasn't telling her. "People break up all the time, and maybe she was agitated about the breakup."

"Maybe, but remember how she didn't come over the night I returned? She also left in a rush the night she came for dinner saying she had something she had to attend to. She's a receptionist. What work could she have at ten o'clock at night?"

"What night was that?" Makenna asked.

"The night the insurance guy was killed."

"Okay, that's a bit of a coincidence, but the fire didn't start until after midnight, so why would she have to rush out?" Makenna had her reservations about Felicity - she had found it odd that his sister hadn't come to see him the first night - but she was not about to accuse someone else in Bubba's family unless the proof was there. So far, there were just some odd coincidences and a general feeling of unease.

Bubba shrugged and shook his head. His hand ran across his chin again. "I don't know. To prepare? Plan it out? Maybe these visions come on suddenly and once she gets one, she has to plan her attack right then."

"It's possible." Makenna chose her words carefully. She didn't want him to think she was dismissing his concern. "However, that's a huge accusation to place on your sister."

Bubba sighed and ran a hand through his hair. "I

know, but she also had a rough childhood and sometimes when she looks at me, it just feels wrong. I hate saying that about her, especially since she's family, but if the killer could be anyone, don't you think we should at least consider the possibility?"

Makenna stared at him. Did he really think his foster sister could be capable of arson and murder? She couldn't quite read the emotion on his face, but she thought it appeared to be a sad determination. "You're right, we'll look into her, but I want to look into the victims first. And I want to go back over the women. Maybe there was something other than you that tied them all together that we missed." She desperately hoped there was something they had missed. Swallowing that would be a lot easier than throwing his family into disarray again.

Half an hour later, they sat at a table with officer Cook who had pulled everything he could find on Dr. Hayworth.

"You might be right, Captain. Dr. Hayworth has some interesting discrepancies between what he charged clients and what he billed to insurance companies. If the companies don't know already, they'll probably be opening an investigation into him soon."

"Wasn't the insurance guy doing a similar thing?" Bubba asked.

Makenna nodded as she thought back over the scene.

"Yeah, he was intercepting checks and telling clients they were denied. Is there any evidence of Peter overcharging clients? We know his ex-girlfriend Skye said he cheated on her, and his mother said he was asking for money."

"Nothing yet, but we're still looking. However, it was his shop. He could have charged people extra and few would realize it."

"Okay, and how about the women?"

Officer Cook shook his head. "I'm not finding anything with money issues or relationship issues with the women. Is it possible we're looking at a copycat?"

Copycat murders happened, but Makenna had a hard time believing they would happen in this small town. They were already dealing with an insanely rare situation. "I won't discount that possibility, but I think it's much more likely that our woman is a visionary who is getting dreams or messages to kill certain people."

She turned to Bubba. "I still think you're the link for the first round, and if so, we could be looking for someone who was interested in you. Maybe someone you turned down or possibly you didn't even know was interested."

Bubba cocked an eyebrow at her. "No offense, but that makes it a pretty impossible list. I can give you the names of the few women I dated, even the ones who I thought were interested that I turned down, but if I didn't know they liked me then, I certainly won't have any idea now."

"That is true. We'll start with what we do know and work backwards from there."

"We better get some coffee then," Bubba said with a smile. "I have a feeling this might be a long day."

CHAPTER 15

*B*ubba kept his eyes peeled for Rachel as they walked to the coffee shop. He still couldn't place how he knew her, but the vibe she had given off the first day combined with the fact that she appeared to be following him made her a woman he wanted a word with.

Unfortunately, she didn't materialize before they reached the shop. Nor did she appear to be inside. Daphne was though, and her face lit up when her eyes landed on Bubba.

"Matt Fisher, back for more?"

"Hey, Daphne." He didn't know why her uber chipper attitude affected him the way it did. Perhaps it was just because she still looked at him the way she had in high school - like she was already picking out curtains and china patterns for their life together - and he didn't want to do anything to make her think there was a future there.

"You want the same coffee you had the other day?"

"You remember what I drank?" He turned slightly to catch Makenna's eye. Was she hearing this?

"Of course I do." She flashed him another wide, flirtatious smile.

"I, uh, think I'll just have an Americano today."

"With two sugars?" she asked, unfazed by his order change.

"Yeah, how did you know that?"

"That's what you drank in high school, Matt. I told you, I remember everything." Her smile was still bright, but for a moment, he thought he saw her eyes flicker. Change. As if for just an instant, something dark crossed her mind.

"Right, of course." He grabbed his wallet to pay for the drink, but as she rang up the order, he noticed the bandage on her hand. "What happened to your hand, Daphne?"

"Oh, this? Burned it on the coffee machine this morning," she said with a laugh. "I'm such a klutz sometimes."

He did remember Daphne being klutzy occasionally in high school except when she was cheering or performing on stage which he always found odd. She could trip over a speck of dirt in the hallway, but when pom poms were in her hands or lights were on her, she seemed to have the focus of a surgeon. Still, was she telling the truth? He couldn't imagine Daphne hurting anyone, but it was odd that her hand was injured the night after someone bled on a rock at a crime scene. He wondered if Felicity would have a cut? Or Rachel?

Shaking his head, he handed over his money and shuffled down to the end of the counter to wait for his drink. He had to stop thinking about Felicity like a suspect. She was probably completely innocent and he was simply chasing shadows that didn't exist.

As he waited for his drink and for Makenna, he scanned the room again. He felt eyes on him, and there by the door, he saw her. Rachel. The mystery woman. His eyes widened, but before he could move, she bolted out the door.

"Where are you going?" Makenna called after him as he made his way through the crowded tables to the door.

"Be right back." He pushed open the door and scanned the area. To the left were the other businesses but no sign of the woman. He turned right, but it too was void of people. It was like she had vanished into thin air. Where could she have gone?

With a sigh, he returned to the shop. Makenna stood at the end of the counter with two drinks in her hands. "What was that about?" she asked, holding out his cup.

Bubba glanced back at Daphne who appeared engaged with a customer. She probably wasn't listening, but he didn't want to take any chances. He shook his head and whispered softly, "Not here. Come on."

She followed him out of the shop and to a bench a few feet away. "You want to tell me what happened in there?"

"I don't know. Maybe I'm going crazy. First there was Daphne who still seems obsessed with me, and for a moment, I thought I saw something in her eyes. Something strange. " He wasn't sure he could put into words the exact feeling. "Plus, did you notice her bandage?"

"I did, but she said she burned it on the coffee machine."

"Maybe she did, but you have to admit, the timing is odd. Then there was that woman, Rachel, but when she saw me, she ran out of the shop. When I got outside, she was nowhere to be seen."

Makenna placed a hand on his arm. "First off, you aren't going crazy. This case has us all tied in knots, and this new information is a lot to process."

He glanced down at her hand on his skin and then back to her eyes. The desire to kiss her burned within him again, but she'd said they had to remain professional. Easy to say but much harder to do. How long had it been since a woman had ignited these feelings in him? But were they real? Or did they simply feel real because of this crazy situation? And even if they were real, what then? He didn't plan to stay here once this case was complete. His life was back in Fire Beach. And did he think she would come back with him? Her life was obviously here. He supposed they could do a long-distance relationship, but he'd been alone for so long that he didn't want to be with someone and not be able to see her. No, kissing her would be a bad idea. He knew that, but then why did he keep thinking about it?

"You're right. I don't know how you do this every day."

Makenna chuckled. "Well, not every day is like this thankfully. Most days, I'm issuing traffic tickets or breaking up fights after a football game or at The Hop. I don't think I'd want to do this every day, but I think you might be onto something. I do want to talk to Daphne and Rachel."

"And Felicity," Bubba added. He still couldn't get the uncomfortable dinner out of his mind.

Makenna removed her hand, and Bubba immediately missed the warmth. "Tell me more about Felicity," she said as they stood and began walking back toward the station. "I don't know her well."

Bubba sighed as he thought of where to begin. "My mom and dad felt a calling to help kids after my brother and sister and I graduated from high school, but they were older, and they knew they couldn't handle small children, so they took in teenagers. Most of the kids didn't last long because by high school, they are generally either too messed up to want a home or they're so independent that they go off on their own as soon as they can.

"Felicity was different. She wanted a home. Evidently, her father had been an alcoholic and beat her and her mother when she was young. Her mother eventually turned to drugs, and her father was killed in a bar fight. She went from one foster home to another until she landed with us.

"She was quiet at first, and because I was older and out of the house, we weren't that close. But when Jacob and Rebecca moved away, I spent more time with her. Still, something was always off. Once or twice, I brought a woman home to meet my parents, and Felicity would issue snide remarks about them under her breath. It almost felt as if she had a crush on me, but maybe she was just looking out for me. Those women didn't last, obviously."

Makenna shook her head as if wanting to make sure he understood. "It wouldn't be the first time a foster kid has developed a misplaced attraction for a sibling. A lot of them mistake romantic feelings for security, which is what they're really craving. Still, given where we're at, it's worth looking into. You said she just broke up with a boyfriend too?"

Bubba nodded. "Yeah, her boyfriend, Roger. She doesn't seem especially torn up about it either which I find odd because Mom said they were together for years."

"Maybe we should talk to Roger."

Bubba nodded. He'd like to meet the man who had dated Felicity himself, see what kind of person he was.

❀❀

*I*t took a stop at Bubba's parents' house to find out who Roger was. Even in this small town, Makenna didn't know everyone's name. Roger turned out to be Roger Ellison who ran the only bed and breakfast in town.

"Felicity? Why are you asking about Felicity?" he asked as he placed the breakfast dishes in the sink.

Makenna looked to Bubba. She wasn't sure just coming out with their suspicions would be the smartest way to handle this. Bubba, thankfully, seemed to understand and took the lead.

"She's my sister. I'm not sure we ever met, but I'm Matt Fisher."

Roger turned to face them, his eyes wide. "I thought you were dead. That's what Felicity told me."

"We needed people to think that," Makenna said, stepping in. "I'm sure you must have heard about the recent fires."

"Yep, kinda hard to miss that." Roger turned back to the sink and turned on the faucet. "Especially in a town of this size."

"Well, we had a similar string of arsons five years ago. Matt here was one of the victims, but he managed to get away. However, to test a theory, we let everyone believe he died."

Roger shut off the water and turned back to them, leaning against the sink. "I assume your theory turned out to be true?"

"It did. Until the fires started again. I asked Matt to come back to help." Makenna was having a hard time reading Roger. Was he guarded because of his feelings for Felicity or was he hiding something?

"I know I've been away from Felicity for several years, but she seems off. We were hoping that maybe you could fill us in on her behavior the last few years you were together and why it ended," Bubba said stepping in.

Roger folded his arms across his chest and sighed. "I'm not sure anything I have to say will help you, but I'll try. Felicity and I met about six months after your "death." I guess I moved to town a month or so after the fires ended, and I worked at a crisis hotline in the evenings while I was getting this place ready. Felicity was grieving and became a regular caller. It's not generally recommended to meet the people you talk to on the phone, but she begged me. I said no at first, but after about a month of phone calls, it appeared she really needed a friend, so we agreed to meet at a coffee shop.

"It was sort of attraction at first meet, I guess you could say. Though I think some of that was because we had shared so much over the phone. Anyway, we started dating, and for a time, everything was great. But then, about a month ago, something changed. She began talking about all the people who came into the office and how she wished she could help them. I think she was reading the doctor's notes on them because she had way too much information."

"Wait," Makenna interrupted him as puzzle pieces began turning in her head, "doesn't she work for a local doctor?"

"Yep, Dr. Bloom, the psychiatrist. She's the receptionist there. Now, maybe these people were sharing while they waited for their appointment, but I don't think so. When I asked her about it, she got defensive and told me to mind my own business. It just went downhill from there, and I finally had to call it off for my own sanity."

Makenna exchanged a glance with Bubba. She didn't want to think his sister could be the arsonist, but she now had motive, odd behavior, and a troubling history.

Roger caught the look and shifted his eyes from Makenna to Bubba. "Is she okay? I mean I couldn't take the negativity, but I still care about her, you know? I know she had it rough growing up."

"We're going to find out, Roger," Makenna said, putting out her hand. "Thank you for your help."

He shook it, but his eyes were on Bubba. "I wish I could do more."

"Thank you, you've helped a lot."

Makenna knew those words were hard for Bubba to say. She thanked Roger again and led the way out of the house. When the front door closed behind them, and she was confident they were out of earshot, she turned to Bubba. "I think you're right. We need to question Felicity." Her list of suspects was growing, but Felicity was at the top of the list right now.

His face was pale, but he nodded. She couldn't imagine how hard this must be on him. If Felicity was the arsonist, it meant not only had she murdered five people but that she'd tried to kill him as well. That had to be hard to swallow.

CHAPTER 16

*T*he ride to Dr. Bloom's office was quiet, uncomfortable. What would his mother say if she knew he was on his way to pick up his sister on suspicion of murder?

"What can you tell me about Rachel Hanes?" Bubba asked, trying to get his mind off the task at hand. He still couldn't shake the feeling that he knew her somehow and that she was important.

"Um, I don't know much about her. She's a little odd, but she stays out of people's way. She's been here as long as I can remember, so maybe you crossed paths with her before?"

"Yeah, that's what I've been trying to figure out. She doesn't look familiar to me, but the name does." He ran again through the list he had started in his head. He didn't remember saving her, but he certainly didn't remember every victim's name from five years ago. Sometimes he never even knew their names. He'd never dated a Rachel, and he was sure he would remember her if he had.

So, that left high school. Had he known a Rachel in high school? He ran through the names and faces he did remember, but there was no Rachel Hanes. But there had been a Rachel. Rachel….Rachel Jones? He hadn't known her well, but he remembered the name from a musical program. He'd only ever been to one and only then because his best friend had asked him to go because he was dating one of the actresses. It had turned out to be a nightmare because Daphne had also been in that cast, and she'd been convinced Bubba had been there to see her. It had taken weeks to convince her otherwise. Could it be the same Rachel? Could she and Daphne be in on this together?

"Do you know if Rachel Hanes is married or was married?"

"I don't know for sure, Bubba, but I promise you if Felicity turns out not to be our suspect that we'll look into her, okay?"

Bubba nodded, but he couldn't shake the feeling that held on with claws and wouldn't let go.

"You sure you want to come in?" Makenna asked when they reached the office. She turned off the engine and shifted so she was facing him. "You don't have to."

He appreciated her concern, but he had to know. If his sister had really tried to kill him, he needed to be there when she was confronted. "No, I'm good."

Concern flashed in Makenna's eyes, but she nodded. "Okay, let's go."

Bubba's heart pounded in his chest as they approached the office door. Would Felicity have a cut? Would she try to run? Turn herself in? Questions and scenarios flashed through his mind, but he had no way to prepare for the unknown.

Makenna pulled open the door and entered first. Bubba almost ran into her when she stopped short in the room. He scanned to see what had made her pause and realized the woman manning the receptionist desk was not his sister, but a petite blond.

"Can I help you?" she asked when she ended the call she was on and looked up at them.

"We're looking for Felicity Fisher," Makenna said.

The girl shrugged. "Sorry, she's not here today. Called in sick. I'm Becky, the temp. Is there anything I can do for you?"

"Is Dr. Bloom available? You can tell him it's Captain Drake," Makenna asked.

"Her, you mean. Dr. Bloom is a woman."

"Of course, my mistake." Makenna recovered nicely,

but Bubba could see that this information had thrown her. It had thrown him too. He wasn't sure why, but he had also assumed Dr. Bloom was a man.

"Let me check." The woman punched a button on the phone and waited. "Dr. Bloom, there's a Captain Drake and a man here to see you. Do you have a moment?" She looked up at them and nodded. "Yes, ma'am." She replaced the phone and motioned them toward the door. "She said to go on in."

"Thank you." As Makenna led the way to the office, Bubba wondered what she had up her sleeves. Was she just hoping to get more information or did she think Felicity might be hiding in Dr. Bloom's office?

"Captain Drake, what can I do for you?" Dr. Bloom was a smart looking woman with her dark hair pulled back in a severe bun, and a pair of cat-eyed glasses that accentuated her thin cheekbones. She sat behind her desk, and Bubba found it odd that she didn't rise to greet them.

"I was hoping to ask you a few questions about your employee, Felicity Fisher."

Dr. Bloom's eyes shifted to Bubba and a tingle ran down his spine. Why was she looking at him like that? Did he know her? He certainly didn't remember ever meeting her before.

"This is my friend and Felicity's brother, Matt Fisher," Makenna said.

"Ah, yes, Felicity told me about your faked death. You know it took quite a toll on her. Losing you." Her eyes bored into his, and the concern she was projecting felt a lot more like blame to him.

"I know, but we thought it was the right move at the time," Bubba said.

"Fair enough, so how can I help?" She leaned forward and placed her hands on the desk, one on top of the other.

"Did you speak with Felicity today?" Makenna asked.

"No, we have a temp agency who fills her spot when she is sick. She must have called them directly."

"Is she sick often?"

"Rarely. She's very punctual and efficient."

"She recently broke up with her boyfriend and he said her behavior had changed recently. Have you noticed anything different lately?"

Dr. Bloom shrugged. "This can be a challenging job. Felicity has to listen to people in the waiting room and deal with customers on the phone. She handles it well though perhaps she's been a bit more short tempered than normal."

"Does she have access to your files? Her boyfriend also stated she seemed to have knowledge of cases."

At this Makenna finally seemed to find the chink in the doctor's stoic demeanor, and her laid back attitude disappeared. "No, I do all my notations online. She would have no reason to know anything about my cases unless the clients told her themselves. I'm assuming you're not just here about that though, am I right?"

"No, I'm afraid Felicity is a person of interest in a current case."

A person of interest was putting it mildly in Bubba's mind. She was their number one suspect, but perhaps Makenna was downplaying it for a reason.

"You think she's the arsonist?" The doctor shook her head slowly as if she were considering this option for the first time. "She does have some of the markers: abuse in her past, a recent trigger, but I think you're wrong about Felicity. I don't know why she was in my files, but I don't believe she's your arsonist."

"With all due respect, ma'am, that's for me to determine. Do you have Felicity's current address?"

"Of course." The doctor turned to her computer and tapped a few keys, but Bubba noticed she only used her left hand. Strange. Someone who typed as much as she claimed to surely didn't chicken peck the notes. Perhaps she used voice to text? "Her address is 1214 Sway Ave. She's not your killer though."

"I hope you're right. Thank you." Makenna nodded at the doctor and led the way out of the office.

Bubba followed, wanting to hear her take on what had just happened, but he held his question until they were back in her car. "Did Dr. Bloom seem a little off to you?"

Makenna shook her head. "Off how?"

"I don't know. The way she looked at me, the fact that she only typed with one hand. What kind of a doctor only uses one hand to type? Did you see her right hand at all?"

"She placed both hands on the desk," Makenna said.

"Yes, but she had the left over the right."

"Bubba, I think you're hoping to find something that proves it's not Felicity, but blaming Dr. Bloom is a bit of a stretch. What's the motive? She's a psychiatrist who helps people."

"Maybe they were all clients. Did you look into that?" He didn't want Felicity to be the arsonist, but that wasn't what this was about. Something about Dr. Bloom had seemed wrong to him. Maybe it was just them showing up unannounced and maybe it was learning about Felicity. But maybe it was something more.

Makenna opened her mouth and then sighed before speaking. "Okay, we didn't look into counseling. We can check that. After we talk to Felicity."

"The doctor seemed certain Felicity isn't the suspect. She's a psychiatrist. Wouldn't she know?"

"It's possible, but she's not her psychiatrist, Bubba. She's Felicity's boss which means she has a different relationship with her."

"So, what now?"

"Now, we go to Felicity's house and hope we can find her before anyone else ends up dead."

❀

She paced around the room, trying to calm her rage. Failure was not an option and yet she had failed. Again. She pulled out the pictures of her victims, landing on Matt Fisher. This was his fault. His appearance in town had thrown her off her game. He was not supposed to have survived. No one was supposed to survive. So, the only thing to do was get rid of him. Then she would see clearly again.

But how? How could she take out Matt when he was always with Captain Drake? The station? They were bound to be spending time together there, but could she set the station on fire? The station would have surveillance cameras. If she did this, she would have to leave town, which meant she might not be able to finish the Dr. Hayworth mission.

"What do I do?" she asked aloud. The voice had been curiously silent today. Was he angry that she failed?

"Let it go," the wimpy voice whispered.

"Shut up," she yelled at the voice. "You are a coward. You are worthless."

The voice stilled, and while she felt satisfaction at that, she still wasn't getting the orders she needed. But that was okay. She could wait. If she'd learned nothing else over the years, she had learned patience, and she could wait. But not here. She couldn't think with the two men smiling at her. Mocking her failure. She had to get out and clear her head. Then he would tell her what to do. She was sure of it.

❦

*M*akenna wished she had the words to say to Bubba as they drove to Felicity's house, but what did you say to someone when you were about to arrest his sister?

"You don't have to go in with me," Makenna said when she pulled the car to a stop in front of the small rambler. "I could leave you here and get her without you."

Bubba shook his head, but his eyes remained fixed out the window. "No, if she is responsible, I want to be there. In some weird way, I feel like I owe her, like I failed her somehow."

Makenna touched his arm and waited to speak until he turned to face her. "You did not fail her, Bubba. If she is the arsonist, her parents failed her long before she ever met you."

He squeezed her hand and held her gaze a moment. "Thank you."

His touch sent a tremor down her spine, and her throat dried up as if she'd swallowed a cotton ball by mistake. "You're welcome," she said softly, pushing the words past the cotton. "I guess we better go." It wasn't what she wanted to say. She wanted to tell him she enjoyed his company, that she hoped they could have a future, that she didn't want to be just friends. However, now was not the time. It could wait until they found the killer.

He let go of her hand, and with great reluctance, she dropped her hand from his arm and opened her car door.

The house was dark as they approached, and Makenna wondered briefly if they were walking into a trap. Would Felicity lure them here and then set her own house on fire? Makenna's hand touched the butt of her gun, but it wouldn't be much help against a fire.

Her blood pulsed in her ears like a rhythmic beating of a drum, but she forced her breathing to stay even. It wasn't dark yet. The killer always struck after dark, so surely they would be safe. She hoped they would be safe. She'd promised Bubba's parents she would protect him, yet here she was dragging him along to danger.

The porch creaked under her feet, and the hairs on her neck lifted, but then she felt Bubba's calming presence behind her. He placed a hand on the small of her back, and her heart began to slow. After a deep breath, she pressed the bell. The chime echoed throughout but then silence fell again.

"Maybe she's not home?" Bubba asked as the silence drew out.

"Do you know where she might go?" Makenna didn't have a warrant, so she couldn't just bust into the house, and the blinds were pulled, blocking visibility.

"No, but my parents might."

Makenna sighed. "I didn't want to get your parents involved, but you're right. They're probably our best hope." She just hoped they would talk to her when they found out what she wanted.

CHAPTER 17

*B*ubba shivered as he opened the car door and stepped out into the cool evening. Night was approaching, sending shadows across the streets, and he felt eyes on him. He looked down the street, but he could see nothing. He must just be on edge.

There was no need to knock, but Bubba paused a moment at the door anyway. What would his parents say when they told them why they were here? Would this damage the relationship he had just begun to rebuild?

"You okay?" Makenna asked. She might have said she wanted to remain strictly personal but her eyes brimmed with concern. They would have to revisit this relationship when the killer was safely behind bars.

"Yeah, just wishing she wasn't a suspect."

"Me too, but it will be all right." She placed a hand

on his arm, and Bubba forced himself to focus on the task at hand and not how much he wanted to kiss Makenna. *After*, he told himself. *When everyone is safe again. Then we can think about the future.*

He pushed the door open, calling for his mother as he stepped over the threshold.

"Captain Drake, nice to see you again," his mother said as she rounded the corner, but her tone didn't match her words. She sounded about as happy to see Makenna as she would be to invite a tax collector in for an audit. Bubba couldn't blame her. Makenna seemed to bring bad news whenever she showed up around here.

"You as well, Margaret. Mind if I come in?"

"Well, you're here already." His mother turned and led the way into the living room.

"Felicity, what are you doing here?" Bubba asked as he rounded the corner and saw his sister curled up on the couch.

"She's been here all day," his mother said as she reached down to touch Felicity's head. "She called a little after you left this morning. She's running a fever and needed someone to take care of her, so I brought her here. Why?"

"We were actually looking for Felicity," Makenna said. "We need to ask her a few questions."

His mother crossed her arms, and her mouth pulled

into a tight line. She moved as if to shield Felicity. "Don't tell me you think Felicity is the arsonist now."

Oh no, this was going downhill quickly. He could see the 'mama bear' instincts taking over, and he needed to pacify her if they had any hope of getting their questions answered. "There's some information that needs clarifying, Mom."

"I'll answer their questions," Felicity said, struggling to sit up a bit.

Bubba scanned her for any sign of a cut, but he could see nothing. He shot Makenna a look hoping she would notice the same.

"You don't have to," his mother said. "I'm sure Captain Drake knows you have the right to an attorney."

"It's fine, Mom." Felicity placed a hand on their mother's arm which seemed to quell her intensity. For the moment at least. Bubba nodded to Makenna. It was now or never.

Makenna cleared her throat, obviously nervous having to ask these questions in front of their mother. "Felicity, we spoke to Roger earlier, and he said you changed in the last month, grew more negative and began talking about helping the people who came into the office. Can you tell me why the sudden change?"

Felicity took a deep breath and let it out slowly. "A month ago, I got a call from a doctor in Richmond. I guess my biological mother ended up there a few years ago. I hadn't heard anything from her since Child Protective Services pulled me from her house so long ago, but I guess they found her unconscious on a park bench. She never woke up, and this doctor was calling to tell me that she passed away. So yeah, things changed for me a month ago. I had a lot of memories dredged up."

"Why didn't you tell us?" his mother asked as she sat on the edge of the couch next to Felicity.

"I didn't want to bother anybody with it. You all have been so good to me, but when the memories came flooding back, I just felt like I needed to help the people I saw everyday. I mean they come in once a week, and it doesn't seem as if Dr. Bloom is doing anything for them.

"Sometimes they would tell me their stories as they waited for their appointment, and sometimes I would hear things as I walked by the room. I didn't mean to look in their case files, I just thought maybe I could help them if I knew more about their issues. If they had backgrounds like mine."

"Felicity, I have to ask, where were you last night?" Makenna still sounded all business, but Bubba could hear the compassion in her voice.

"I was home all night. Why?"

"There was another arson last night, and we think the person was injured. Can I see both of your arms?"

Felicity held her arms up, but there were no cuts, no bandaids. Where did this leave them now?

"Satisfied?" his mother asked.

"Yes, ma'am. I'm sorry, but I had to ask. Felicity, I know there is a lot in your past, but I'm sure Dr. Bloom would help you process your feelings or find someone who could help you."

"Roger wanted to let you know that he still cares for you as well," Bubba added. "Maybe if you talk to him, explain things, you guys can work it out."

"Thank you both," Felicity said.

Suddenly Bubba wondered if Felicity might know about Rachel Hanes. Maybe she had been a patient or maybe she had just been privy to some gossip. Either way, he figured it was worth a shot. "Felicity, do you know Rachel Hanes?"

"Rachel Hanes," she appeared to think for a moment before nodding. "Yeah, the odd one, right? Always hanging around coffee shops, but never speaking to anyone?"

"Sounds like her. Do you know her story?"

Felicity cocked her head at him. "You don't remember her?"

Bubba blinked at the tone in Felicity's voice. It was obvious she thought he should know her, so why couldn't he remember her. "No, should I? She seems familiar, but I can't place her and I don't remember her name."

"Her husband was the one killed at the construction

site. You told me you watched him die and felt badly you all didn't reach him in time."

Bubba fell into the nearby recliner and ran a hand across his forehead. He'd forgotten all about that incident. Or maybe pushed it from his mind was more like it. It wasn't the only death he'd ever seen, but it had certainly been one of the more gruesome.

"I'm afraid I'm not following," Makenna said. "Can someone fill me in?"

Bubba sighed as the memories flooded his mind. "About a month before the murders started five years ago, the fire department was called out to a construction incident. A worker had been working on the top of a building when the scaffolding he was standing on broke beneath him. He was still holding on when we arrived, but before we could get a ladder to him, his fingers slipped, and he fell to his death. We all watched as the life drained out of him. It was horrible."

"Was Rachel there?" Makenna asked. "Why would she blame you and not the other firemen?"

"I was the one extending the ladder. The story was in the newspaper for the next week, and an investigation was even opened, but I was cleared."

"Well, that is definitely a reason to ask Rachel a few questions," Makenna said. "What could have triggered her now though?"

"I'd have to look to be sure, but I'm fairly certain that

the first recent death would be five years to the day that her husband died."

Before Makenna could respond, the sound of glass shattering carried through the house.

"What was that?" His mother's fearful eyes glanced toward the front of the house.

"Wait here." Bubba raced toward the utility room where the fire extinguisher was stored. He couldn't smell the gas as he rounded the corner, but he knew the fire would not be far behind.

"I'm going after her," Makenna called as she pulled her gun and raced past Bubba and toward the front of the house.

"Be careful," he called, but she was already out of earshot.

🕸

*M*akenna rounded the corner just as the flame erupted. The force of the heat lifted her and flung her back against the wall. Though she didn't lose consciousness, for a moment she also couldn't move. Shock. It had to be shock.

She watched as the flame crept closer to her. Was she going to die here? She needed to get up, but her body refused to cooperate. Then she saw the white foam of the fire extinguisher and Bubba wielding the nozzle with an expert touch.

The fire danced and darted as if trying to avoid capture, but Bubba had been quick, and he had the flame out before it could destroy more of the house.

"Are you okay?" he asked after setting the fire extinguisher down. He knelt down beside her and placed his hands on her cheeks. "Makenna, are you okay?"

Makenna could see his lips moving, enough to make out the words, but all she could hear was ringing. "I'm fine, I think." She felt her mouth moving, but she couldn't even hear her own words. She hoped that he could.

"You need to see a doctor." The words were muffled but she could make them out as the ringing subsided. Bubba's eyes brimmed with concern as his fingers touched her face and then slid down her neck and arms as if searching for injuries.

She knew she did, but she also needed to see if the arsonist was still outside. The chances were slim. Makenna had probably missed her window, but she had to be sure. "Not until I see if she's still here."

Bubba shook his head, and his hands returned to her face. He held her gingerly, and Makenna warmed at the look in his eyes. They were failing miserably at this professional only relationship. "You're in no condition to chase anyone down, and she's probably long gone by now. Let me call an ambulance. None of us can stay here tonight anyway."

Makenna wanted to argue, but her body still wasn't responding the way it should. Instead, she nodded and tried to stand. Bubba moved his hands to her shoulders and pressed gently. "You're not moving until an ambulance arrives to check you out."

A small smile touched her lips. She had suspected he was a protector, and she couldn't deny that it felt nice having someone take care of her. If only he lived closer. If only she could convince him to stay. "Okay, I won't move, but can you click on my radio, so I can call dispatch?"

"Of course." He grabbed the radio from her belt.

Makenna prayed it hadn't been injured in the blast and would still work. Relief flooded her at the sound of the familiar squelch when he pressed the call button. He held it to her mouth. "Dispatch, this is Captain Drake. I need an ambo and a squad car to 353 Fir Street."

"Captain Drake, Matt, are you two okay?" Bubba's mother's voice carried in from the other room.

"We're okay, Mom, but we can't stay here. Pack some clothes and things you and Dad need. We'll find a place to stay for tonight."

"You can stay with me," Makenna said although she wasn't sure Bubba staying in her house was a good idea.

Not with him looking at her like that, and her heart racing the way it was.

He smiled and brushed a strand of hair behind her ear. "I appreciate the offer, Makenna, but I don't think your place will be any safer. If she knows where I live, she probably knows where you live too."

"You're right," Makenna agreed placing her hand on his. She really wished she wasn't injured because the desire to kiss him right now burned throughout her body. "She attacked much earlier than usual, and not in the normal way."

"What do you mean?" Bubba asked.

"Molotov cocktail. The flame exploded when I walked in the room. I bet if you look around, you'll find glass shards. Maybe if we're lucky, we'll find fingerprints on those shards."

Bubba stepped away from her and scanned the floor. A moment later, he leaned over and using the hem of his shirt, he picked something up from the floor. "Looks like you're right."

Makenna marveled at how careful he was with the evidence. He had good instincts. She wondered if she could convince him to cross into police work and stay here with her. "Tad and Kelsey should be here soon. We'll let them deal with the evidence, but we have to figure out somewhere to go."

"You're going to the hospital to get checked out. Maybe we can get some hotel rooms after that."

The front door opened then and Tad and Kelsey burst in. "Captain? Are you okay?"

"I think I'm just shaken up, Tad, but I need to get looked at. Did you see her outside? The arsonist?"

Tad shook his head. "No, there was no one out there."

Makenna nodded. "I figured. We'll find her another way. She used a Molotov cocktail this time. Bubba found one glass shard, but I'm sure there are more. You and Kelsey see what you can find while I'm getting checked out."

"Of course, Captain. And then what?" Kelsey asked.

"Then we need to find a place to stay. No one can stay here, and I don't trust my place or Felicity's."

"I have room at my place," Kelsey offered.

Bubba shook his head. "Kelsey, we couldn't impose."

"Yes, you can. I insist. I'll take you and your family to my house while Captain Drake gets looked at."

Makenna exchanged a glance with Bubba. It wasn't her first choice, but right now, their options were limited.

"No, you can take my family, but I'm going with Makenna."

Tad and Kelsey exchanged a glance, but before they could say anything, the EMTs entered and began strapping Makenna to the board. As they loaded her in the ambulance, she prayed that her injuries weren't serious enough to keep her off the case. More than ever, she needed to find this woman and stop her.

Bubba climbed up beside her and grabbed her hand as the EMT began prepping her arm for an IV.

"We're going to have to talk about this soon," Makenna said, smiling up at him. Something had definitely changed between them, and though she had no idea where it might end up, she was going to enjoy it while it lasted.

He returned her smile and squeezed her hand. "Promise, but let's get you checked out first."

CHAPTER 18

"You didn't have to come with me," Makenna said as Bubba wheeled her out to the waiting police cruiser a few hours later. He hadn't left her side except for when she'd been taken back for x-rays. She'd called Tad to come pick them up only because Bubba didn't have a car with him.

"Yeah, I did. You're tough, Makenna, but everyone has limits, and sometimes I wonder if you know yours. Also, in case you didn't notice, I'd like to keep you around."

Makenna's lips twitched into a lop-sided grin. How did he seem to know her so well in so short a time? "Okay, perhaps you're right. I don't always know when to stop, but all this time we've lost at the hospital?" She shrugged. "I feel like we're running out of time."

"I know, and I feel it too, but I have to trust that God brought us together to catch this woman and that He won't let us fail. However, we have to take care of ourselves to be useful to Him and that means rest and recovery, Makenna."

Makenna nodded at his sage wisdom. She'd been so caught up in following the evidence that she hadn't been bringing it to God, and maybe that was part of the issue.

Tad stepped out of the cruiser as they approached and flashed a tight smile. "Glad to see you're okay, Captain. We got everyone set up at Kelsey's house."

He held out a hand, and Bubba took her other arm. Together, they helped her stand, shuffle the few feet to the car, and slide into the passenger seat. "Good, I think a little sleep is in order, but then I want everyone looking for Rachel Hanes. We think she might be the arsonist, and we need to end this. Today." It was after midnight, so she was counting it as the beginning of the day.

"Understood. I've got Brayden checking on the glass shards. He'll alert us if any fingerprints pop up."

"Good, I'd also like you to find out everything you can about Kevin Hanes's accident from five years ago. I need to know if that's what started all of this, and if it is, what the recent trigger was. Bubba and I will pick up Rachel Hanes tomorrow."

Tad's face pulled into a tight line. "No offense, Captain, but how about you let me pick up Rachel?" Makenna opened her mouth to protest, but Tad held up his hand to stop her and continued. "If she is the killer, who knows what she might do, and you're not in peak condition. I promise I'll bring her straight to the station so you can question her."

"He's right, Makenna," Bubba agreed. "You're going to need to take it slow for a few days."

Makenna knew they were right, but she hated being sidelined especially when she felt they were so close to finally ending it. "Fine. Bubba and I will research, but you ask her nothing without me there."

"Got it." He chuckled and shook his head as he shut her door and walked around to the driver's side.

Ten minutes later, Kelsey met them at her front door. "Welcome to my home," she said, gesturing to the open area behind her. "Patrick, Margaret, and Felicity are all upstairs. Are you ready to do the same?"

Makenna wanted to say no. She wasn't sure she would be getting any sleep tonight anyway, but she had promised Bubba she'd at least try. Who knew what tomorrow would hold. "Yes, let's get some rest, and we can debrief tomorrow morning."

"You got it." As Kelsey led the way up the stairs, Makenna grabbed the railing with one hand and let Bubba offer support with the other. Her eyes scanned the house as she made her way slowly up the steps.

The house was nothing like Kelsey. Filled with knick

knacks and all sorts of kitchy paintings, it was a stark contrast to Kelsey's minimalist attitude. Had she inherited it then? Or had she purchased it this way and just been too busy to make any changes?

"It's a lovely house, Kelsey," Makenna said as they reached the landing. She hated that she was already out of breath.

"Thanks. It was my aunt's which is part of why I moved here. She and I had very different styles, but the structure of the house was so good that I couldn't sell it. One of these days, I'll renovate it though." She opened a door to reveal a pink flowery bedroom. "You can take this one, Captain. Sorry about the pattern."

"It's fine," Makenna said though her stomach was already turning from the assault of flowers on the walls. She squeezed Bubba's arm one last time before closing the bedroom door. They hadn't had their "talk" yet, both agreeing they would rather wait for the case to be over, but Makenna knew strictly professional was no longer an option. She'd felt the change in his touch when he assessed her injuries, and she'd seen it in his eyes both then and on the way to the hospital. The question was what did she do about it?

She changed into a spare shirt Kelsey had and brushed her teeth with an extra toothbrush before climbing into the bed. As she stared at the ceiling, her thoughts alternated between finding the killer and having a heartfelt conversation with Bubba.

She knew she felt something for him, but was it enough to leave her job? Would he ever consider moving here? The questions cycled through her mind, but there would be no answers tonight. Maybe after they caught the killer but not tonight. With a sigh, she closed her eyes and prayed for peace, for safety, and for help in closing this case.

*B*ubba stared at the ceiling in the guest room and tried to process his feelings. It had been a long time since he had opened his heart, but he wanted to. He was tired of being alone, tired of watching his friends find love and trying to live vicariously through them. He'd shut those feelings off for fear he would fall for someone and she would get hurt because of him, but when he'd seen Makenna lying against the wall, he'd been so afraid that she was dead. That she had died before he got to tell her how he felt. He knew his feelings for her had been growing, but he hadn't known how much until then.

And he knew she was feeling something too. He'd seen it in her eyes when he touched her, felt it spark between them, and she'd said they needed to talk in the ambulance. But where did that leave them? Could he come back and live in Woodville and be Matt Fisher again? Would she ever consider leaving? Could they make a long distance relationship work? It was easier with video chats and instant messaging, but they both had demanding jobs. Could they even find times to virtually meet up?

Bubba pulled out his cell phone and opened his Bible App. He usually preferred holding the Bible in his hands - there was something about the feel of it that always gave him comfort - but as he didn't have his Bible, his phone would have to do. He flipped to the book of John and began reading. As he did, he prayed for wisdom. His life had changed so much in the last few days, and he had no idea what he was going to do when the killer was caught. But he did know that God could offer peace, and that was exactly what he needed right now.

❦

*H*ow could she have been so stupid? She never should have gone to Matt's house, and she certainly shouldn't have thrown the bottle in. She'd let her anger get the best of her, and that wasn't smart. She needed to be smart. She needed wisdom. However, the voice was still curiously silent. Had she angered him with her failures? Was he done with her now? What would she do if he stopped talking? Could she let the weak voice take over again?

"Help me," she pleaded with her empty room, but there was no answer. At least not from him.

"Let it go," the coward said. "It's over."

With a snarl, she ripped Matt Fisher's picture off her wall. "No, it's not over until I say it's over. Attacking the house with everyone there was stupid, but attacking one of his family members wouldn't be. And she knew just who to choose. It was almost too easy.

CHAPTER 19

"*D*id we find anything on the glass shards?" Makenna asked Brayden when she entered the police station the next morning. Her body was still stiff and sore, but the sleep had helped a little. Even though it hadn't been enough. She could walk without assistance, but running would be out of the question as would tackling anyone if it were necessary.

Brayden set his coffee mug down and rubbed his eyes. He had been manning the station all night, and she would let him take the rest of the day off to sleep, but she needed an update first.

"Still waiting on the lab, Captain."

She turned to Kelsey and Tad. "Did you find anything else at the scene? Any usable footprints outside?" She had sent them back to Bubba's parents' house after breakfast to see if the killer had left any clues outside that had been missed in the dark the night before.

"Nothing," Kelsey said with a soft shake of her head. "I think we got lucky at Dr. Hayworth's because his sprinkler system had been leaking which made the ground wet. Everywhere else, it's hard and cold and covered with leaves."

Makenna sighed. She had been hoping for better news though she'd expected this outcome. "Okay, so that means it's time to pick up Rachel. Her husband was killed in a construction accident, and Matt was named in the story that came out about it. Kelsey, you and Tad go find her and bring her in. Brayden, go home and get some sleep. Bubba and I will start looking into the Kevin Hanes accident and see if it's the trigger."

"Copy that." Tad grabbed his car keys, and he and Kelsey headed out. Brayden followed a few minutes later.

When they were alone, Bubba touched Makenna's shoulder. "Can I get you anything? Coffee? Tea?"

"Coffee would be great," Makenna said, "but let's just make it here. I don't want to lose any time waiting at a shop."

"Sounds good. Where's the breakroom? I'll go put a pot on."

Makenna pointed down the hall and watched him

leave before collapsing in the chair behind her desk. She sighed and rubbed her head. The hospital had cleared her last night, but she didn't feel quite right. A chill that she couldn't seem to shake grew inside her, her head still ached, and her back was sore from hitting the wall.

Rest would probably cure all of that, but there was no time for rest now. Their killer was obviously escalating. Four attacks in less than a week and the addition of Molotov cocktails meant she could be spiraling out of control, and if that happened, who knew what she might do next.

Makenna turned on her laptop and began searching for any information on Kevin Hanes.

Bubba returned a few minutes later and held a steaming mug out to her. "I put a little cream and two sugars. I think that's how you drink it, am I right?"

"Right as rain." Makenna took the mug and smiled up at him. It had only been a week, but he already seemed to know her inside and out. She wrapped her hands around her mug to infuse the heat into her hands.

"You have a laptop for me?" Bubba asked as he pulled up a chair to the other side of her desk and sat down.

"You can grab Brayden's. It should be ready to use."

He nodded and returned a moment later with Brayden's laptop. For a few minutes, there was only the sound of tapping keys and the occasional sip from a mug. Makenna marveled at how comfortable she was around Bubba. There was no need to fill the silence with idle chatter.

"It seems I was right about the date," Bubba said. "Here's the original story and the date of the construction accident was five years to the day that the repair shop owner was killed."

"Okay, so that could have been the trigger. Let's see if we can find anything else about Kevin or Rachel." Her hand shook as she picked up the mug again.

*B*ubba tried to keep his focus on the research, but he couldn't help his eyes wandering to Makenna every few minutes. Though she said she was fine, he could tell she wasn't quite herself.

Not only did she still have the dark circles under eyes, but she shivered every few minutes. Was she even aware she was doing it? In addition, she kept picking up her mug and cradling it in her hands even though she didn't always drink it, and occasionally her hand would shake enough to send the coffee sloshing over the lip of the mug. She needed rest, but she was stubborn. He knew she wouldn't take any until this case was over. So, he needed to make sure this ended. Today.

He clicked out of the story of Kevin's accident and

focused on Rachel instead. Who was she? There wasn't much on her other than the fact that she used to be a teacher at the local school before Kevin died. After, it appeared she stopped teaching and withdrew from life. Their marriage certificate showed they hadn't been married long, and he could find no birth certificate for children. Bubba knew death affected people in different ways, but he just couldn't find anything other than Kevin's death that would point to Rachel's behavior.

The door opened, and he looked up to see Kelsey and Tad leading Rachel into the station. She appeared to be calm and collected. At least until she saw him.

"What's he doing here?" she shouted as she charged his direction.

Tad managed to grab her before she reached Bubba, but she struggled against his grip.

"Let me go. He killed my husband," she said as she twisted and writhed.

Tad pulled out his handcuffs and secured her wrists. "Is that why you tried to kill him?"

"Kill him? What are you talking about? Are you listening to me? He killed my husband."

"I didn't kill him, Rachel," Bubba said. His heart broke for her even though he knew he wasn't at fault. "We just didn't get there in time."

"You lie," she spat. "She told me you would, but you were supposed to be dead." Rachel's voice quieted, and she began to rock from side to side. "She told me you were dead."

Makenna and Bubba exchanged glances. He had expected crazy, but this was beyond what he had imagined.

"Who told you Matt was dead?" Makenna asked.

"She told me it would be okay. That he got what he deserved." Her voice was even softer as if she were speaking more to herself than any of them. "But he didn't. He didn't get what he deserved."

"Who, Rachel? Who told you he would get what he deserved?"

Rachel lifted her head and looked at Makenna, but her glazed eyes were clearly seeing something else far away. "Iris."

"Who's Iris?" Kelsey asked.

What was going on here? They'd all thought Rachel was the killer, but now she was rambling about some other woman.

"Rachel," Makenna shook the woman's shoulders. "Who's Iris?"

Rachel blinked as if seeing Makenna for the first time. "His sister," she said before she floated away again.

"His sister?" Tad asked. "Who's sister?"

"Not mine," Bubba said. "Felicity is my foster sister and Rebecca is my biological sister. Could she mean

Kevin?" He looked back at his laptop screen and pulled up Kevin's birth record. "Makenna, come look at this."

Makenna leaned over Bubba's shoulder to read the screen. "He had a twin sister?" Her mouth pulled into a tight line, and though she said nothing, Bubba could read the thought in her head. A twin sister would have a close tie to Kevin and therefore a high chance of wanting revenge on his killer. The question was where was Iris now?

⚜

*M*akenna pulled her gaze away from the screen to issue orders. "Tad, take Rachel to an interrogation room. See what you can find out. Kelsey, Bubba, find out anything you can on Iris Hanes. I need to know where she is."

Silence invaded the room as everyone focused on the task. Bubba typed Iris Hanes into the search bar and began scanning the stories for any clue, any picture.

"I found something, Captain," Kelsey said. "It's a few years old, but this appears to be a picture of Iris Hanes at some conference a few towns over."

Kelsey turned the screen around, and Makenna sucked in her breath. "Bubba, is this who I think it is?" The hair was down and flowing in the picture and the face was younger and graced with a smile, but she would bet her job it was the same woman.

Bubba stared at the picture and nodded. "It sure looks like her."

"Can I buy a clue here?" Kelsey asked. "I feel like I'm missing something."

"Kelsey, I want you to find out everything you can about Dr. Bloom. I want her history all the way back to birth."

"Wait, Dr. Bloom?" Kelsey asked. "Why are we looking into her? I thought we were focused on Iris Hanes."

"Bubba and I are pretty sure that Dr. Bloom is Iris Hanes."

Kelsey's eyes widened and without another word, her face returned to her laptop screen.

"Makenna." Bubba's serious tone grabbed her attention, and she turned his direction. "Did Felicity go to work today?"

A cold sensation flooded Makenna's veins. If Felicity had gone to work today, she could be in real trouble. "Kelsey, keep looking. Call me with anything you find. Bubba, you're with me. Let's go pay Dr. Bloom a visit."

"Makenna, should we bring Tad?" Bubba whispered as they neared the front door.

She knew his words were coming from a place of concern, but they annoyed her all the same. She was fine, and they had no time to bicker about her health. "I'll call him on the way. Let's go."

As they pulled up to Dr. Bloom's office though, Makenna wondered if she had made a mistake not waiting for Tad. There were no other cars in the parking lot which led her to believe that Dr. Bloom was expecting them. Plus, she had no idea what the woman might be armed with, and as much as she wanted to believe she was, Makenna knew she wasn't functioning at one hundred percent. Still, time was of the essence. Especially if Dr. Bloom had Felicity. Who knew what the woman might do.

"You ready?"

Bubba nodded, his face set in a grim determination. Makenna was glad to have him with her even if he wasn't a trained cop. Besides, she knew Tad was on his way. She'd radioed him on the drive over. All she had to do was either take Dr. Bloom in easy, if she acquiesced, or kill a little time until her backup showed up.

"Let's go."

Makenna pulled her gun as she led the way up the sidewalk. She dared a glance in the glass door before she opened it, but the lobby was empty. Either Dr. Bloom wasn't here or she was in her office. Makenna hoped for the latter; she didn't feel like tracking this woman down all over town.

She gestured for Bubba to follow her and then eased her way toward the office door.

"Come on in, Captain Drake. We've been expecting you." The voice that came out of the office sounded little like the Dr. Bloom they had spoken to the day before. Confidence and disdain oozed from this voice, and Makenna did not miss the use of the word we. So, she definitely had someone in there with her.

Makenna stepped into the office. Her gun found Dr. Bloom, but as she had feared, Dr. Bloom was not alone. Felicity sat in the doctor's chair, a knife to her throat and fear burning in her eyes.

"Matt, I know you're out there too. Why don't you join us?"

Makenna hoped Bubba would keep his calm when he saw his sister. The last thing she needed was for someone to get antsy. She felt him fill the space behind her and sensed his tension.

"Iris, this is over. It's time to let Felicity go," Makenna said, trying to take control of the situation.

Iris smiled a cold, calculated smile. "I don't think so. See, I made a mistake once when I didn't make sure Matt here was dead, but he forgave me and granted me a second chance."

He? Who was she talking about. "Do you mean Kevin forgave you?"

"No, not Kevin," Iris laughed, "though I'm sure he

will thank me for bringing his killer to justice. There won't be a mistake this time."

Felicity winced as Iris pulled the knife tighter against her neck. Makenna had no shot. Not with Iris leaning so close to Felicity, but there was a window behind her. If only she could find a way to let Tad know their situation.

"I didn't kill him, Iris," Bubba said, stepping forward. "I was cleared in the investigation. We simply got there too late."

Iris turned her attention to Bubba, and hatred flashed in her eyes. "I felt him die. Did you know that? Twins are connected that way sometimes, and Kevin was my best friend growing up. I was in the middle of a session with a client at my old practice, and I felt this crazy fear come over me. Fear that I was going to die. My lungs closed up and my pulse raced just like his must have.

"And when his heart stopped beating-" Her hand shook and she paused to compose herself. "When his heart stopped beating, mine did too for just an instant, and then I knew that he was gone and this terrible vacantness settled on me."

As Iris got lost in her story, her face turned away from Makenna, and Makenna used that moment to click the talk button on her radio and wedge it into a locked position against her belt so that Tad, Kelsey, and dispatch would hear what was going on. Perhaps it would give them some edge.

"I am incredibly sorry for your loss," Bubba said, taking another step closer to the desk, "but those women you killed were also somebody's sister, somebody's daughter. Their families are now grieving the same as you are."

Iris shook her head. "I should have picked them better. Their deaths were supposed to hurt you. He told me they would, but I didn't choose the right ones. I should have picked Felicity here the first time and maybe your mother, but he wasn't clear. He should have been clear." The hand holding the knife shook, and Felicity whimpered again.

Makenna could see Iris unraveling. She wondered if the doctor even recognized her own psychotic break. "Who is he, Iris? Who's been telling you to kill people?"

Iris turned back to Makenna, and for a moment she looked confused, but then she twitched and the icy face returned. "God, of course. God chose me as his angel. He showed me what to do and gave me the information on them. They were evil people, and they deserved to die."

Makenna shook her head. "No, Iris. They were children of God, made in His image. They might have been doing evil things, but God - the true God - does not condone murder, and He believes in second chances. Even for you."

"I don't need a second chance." Iris's voice rose in pitch and volume. "I was doing His will."

"No, you weren't. Have you heard of a visionary before, Dr. Bloom?" Makenna had no idea if switching to the woman's professional title would cause that part of her to take over, but she had to try.

"Of course I've heard of a visionary," Iris said. "I am a psychiatrist."

"Then you must know that usually those visions are the result of a trauma the patient has experienced. Abuse. Sickness. Death."

Recognition flashed in Dr. Bloom's eyes, and then she twitched again. "No, I'm not a visionary. I'm an angel. There's a difference."

"But you didn't become an angel until Kevin's death, did you?" Makenna pressed. She glanced over at Bubba who was watching, waiting for a sign. She nodded slightly at Felicity, hoping he would understand her message. If she could get Dr. Bloom back, they might have a second to take her down. But only a second.

"I.... no, that's different."

But Makenna could hear the confusion in Dr. Bloom's voice. "Dr. Bloom, the anniversary of Kevin's death was your trigger. It's what brought the visions back. It's when he began talking again, am I right?"

And there it was. Makenna might have missed it if she hadn't been paying close enough attention. She saw the change come over Dr. Bloom a moment before she stepped back.

She stared at Felicity and then the knife in her hands. "What have I done?"

She didn't even have to signal Bubba. With those words, he launched himself across the remaining space, sending Dr. Bloom crashing to the ground and the knife skidding in the other direction. By the time Iris took over again, Bubba had her pinned to the floor, and Makenna was slapping handcuffs on her wrists.

"No, I can't fail him again. I won't."

"Iris Bloom, you have the right to remain silent. Anything you say can and will be used against you in a court of law." Before she finished the Miranda rights, Tad appeared in the doorway, and she passed the woman off to him so she could check on Felicity and Bubba. "Are you okay?"

Felicity was still rubbing her neck, and a thin trickle of blood oozed out of a small cut, but she managed a nod. "Yeah, I'm okay, but I think I'm going to need a new job."

Makenna felt the chuckle bubble inside her, and she caught Bubba's eye and smiled. "Yeah, it looks like you might."

As the three waited for the EMT to arrive and check

Felicity out, Makenna breathed a sigh of relief. It was finally over. She could rest and return to her normal life. But did she want to? She loved her job, but her normal life meant evenings home alone with her cat. It meant paperwork, few dates, legal jargon, and death. And she was no longer sure that was what she wanted.

Watching Bubba with his sister and with his parents these last few days had reminded her of family - the importance of it and what she was missing. Could she give this up though? Running a department had been her dream. Hadn't it? Or had she told herself it was her dream when she'd been shoved into it? She just didn't know.

CHAPTER 20

ubba turned to Makenna as the EMTs carried Felicity out. Though she'd stated she wasn't injured and just wanted to return to Kelsey's to rest, the paramedics had insisted she get her neck looked at. Evidently Iris had pressed hard enough to draw blood at least once, and they wanted to be sure she hadn't damaged anything underneath the skin.

"Reckon we should have that talk now?" he asked as he took Makenna's hand and pulled her to him.

She smiled and wrapped her arms around his neck. "I suppose we should."

Man, how he wanted to kiss her, but he needed to tell her what was on his heart first. "Makenna, after the first murders, I felt such guilt that I didn't think I'd ever open my heart to anyone again, but there is something about you that makes me feel complete, whole. My life isn't here any longer, and I know that yours is, but Fire Beach isn't that far. We could talk during the week and trade weekends."

She shook her head and placed a finger on his lips. "I don't want just weekends, Bubba. I worked hard to get to where I'm at, but I realized last night that my job, my title, means nothing if I don't have someone to share it with."

Bubba wasn't sure what she was saying. Was she telling him it would never work? Or was she saying that she would consider leaving Woodville? "Makenna, it's been a long time since I had to decode woman-speak. Can you just tell me what you mean?"

Makenna laughed and pulled his face down to hers. She placed her lips on his, and even though he still had questions, his arms wrapped around her waist. The kiss was everything he had imagined it would be, and while he had kissed women in the past, those kisses had never felt like this one. This one shook him to the core.

"What I'm saying," Makenna said as she pulled back, "is that this town holds a lot of memories for me. Some are good, but a lot of them I'd rather forget. Now, it might take awhile and I would certainly like to check the place out before I decide completely, but I don't think I would be opposed to transferring to a new police department."

Relief and elation flooded Bubba's body. "Like Fire Beach?"

"Like Fire Beach," she said with a smile, "or anywhere close to it."

"Yes." He picked her up and spun her around before setting her back down and finding her lips once again.

Makenna shivered as Bubba kissed her again. She wasn't sure if it was from the blast the night before or the heat racing through her from his kiss, but she knew that as much as she wanted to stay right here in his arms, she needed rest.

"You're still shivering, Makenna." Bubba's eyes were full of concern as he pulled back this time. "Are you okay?"

"Honestly, I think it's just my body realizing it's all finally over. What do you say we go tell your parents the killer is behind bars and then catch up on the sleep we've been missing this last week?"

"I can't think of anything I'd rather do," he said with a smile.

As they walked out of Iris Bloom's office hand in hand, Makenna thought about all the things she still had to do. She needed to inform the families of the victims that the killer had been caught, she needed to make sure

Iris Bloom was processed correctly, and she needed to look into a replacement. Tad seemed like the obvious choice, but would he want the position? It was definitely a lot of work, but he was young enough and still single. And she couldn't think of anyone else she'd rather pass the mantle off to.

"Captain Drake, Matt, can I get a word?"

Makenna sighed at the sound of Natasha's voice. She was definitely not up to dealing with the reporter. "What are you doing here, Natasha? How did you even know we were here?"

Natasha rolled her eyes and shook her head. "You really don't know what a valuable asset you have, do you? Old Henry is almost always sitting outside your station, and he sees and hears a lot. I paid him a hundred bucks to come find me whenever you left. He wasn't sure where you'd gone, but he remembered the name Felicity, so I figured this was worth a shot."

Old Henry. Makenna should have known. Though the man often had a bottle in hand, Makenna had seen the sharp focus the few times she'd seen him sober. Natasha must have as well and used that to her advantage.

"Is it true then? Dr. Bloom is the killer?"

"It certainly appears that way. Of course, we still have to question her, but she had a knife to Felicity's throat, and she didn't deny the accusation. There's still a long road ahead, but I think the people of Woodville are safe again."

Natasha's eyes dropped to the ground, and she cleared her throat. "It would seem, then, that I owe you an apology, Matt. I'm sorry I threatened to print that first story, and for what it's worth, I'm glad to know it wasn't you."

Makenna stared at the woman in front of her. Had Natasha Kingston actually apologized? By the shocked expression on Bubba's face, she could tell he was having a hard time processing it as well.

"Uh, thank you, I think," he said.

"You're welcome." And then suddenly her apologetic demeanor was gone, and her vicious, cutthroat side reappeared. "Don't think you're getting off so easy when it comes to your relationship though. It's clear there's something going on between the two of you, and I think the people of Woodville could use a feel good story, don't you?" With that, she snapped a picture of the two of them, smiled, and clopped away.

"What just happened?" Bubba asked as if he had just received an unknown error message on a computer.

"I think the world might have just ended," Makenna said with a laugh. It felt good to laugh, to finally relax, and to do it with Bubba.

CHAPTER 21

"*A*re you sure you can't stay a little longer?" his mother asked as Bubba zipped his bag up. He knew that she was asking because she missed him, but he'd already been in Woodville much longer than he'd intended. Thankfully, his captain had agreed to the extra time though Bubba was sure kitchen duty would be on his plate for the next month to make up for it.

"I have to get back, Mom. My life is in Fire Beach now, but I promise I will call and visit." He had stayed the extra few days to make sure their window was repaired and the damaged floor replaced.

"I know it is. It's just been so nice having you here, and there's this part of me that fears if you leave, I'll never see you again."

He stepped away from his bag and took her hands in

his. "Mom, I promise that you will see me again. How about you, Felicity, and Dad come out this weekend to Fire Beach? I'll show you around and you can meet all of my friends. Maybe we can even convince Jacob and Rebecca to come. It can be like a mini family reunion."

His mother sniffed and nodded. "I'd like that. I know you're not little any more, but you'll always be my little boy."

And he wouldn't have it any other way. It was nice to have his family in his life again. "There's just one thing, Mom. My friends all call me Bubba or Billy since that's how they've known me for the last five years."

His mother's nose wrinkled. "Bubba? What kind of a name is that? What's wrong with the name we gave you?"

"It's a nickname, Mom, and I couldn't go by Matt when I first got there. I had to be someone else, remember?"

"Can I still call you Matt?"

"Of course, Mom. You can always call me Matt."

"How about me?" Felicity asked, poking her head in the doorway. She too looked like a new woman. After the hospital released her, Roger had come by to see her. They still had a lot of work to do, but once he heard the reason for her behavior, they had agreed to attend counseling and give their relationship another shot. She still didn't have a new job, but Kelsey had promised to help her find one that would allow her to go to school and get the counseling degree she'd decided she wanted. Bubba had no doubt she would make a fantastic counselor, especially with her ability to relate to people from challenging backgrounds.

"Yes, you can call me Matt too."

"I can't thank you enough, Matt, for saving me, for bringing Roger back into my life, for everything really."

"Hey, that's what big brothers are for," he said as he pulled her in for a hug.

"Yeah, well, don't be a stranger."

"I promise," he said before picking up his bag again. His mother and sister followed him to the front door where his father was waiting. He was not one for embracing his emotions, but Bubba would miss him all the same. "Dad, it was good to see you again."

Bubba stuck out his hand to shake with his father, but his father stared at his hand and then pulled him in for a hug instead. "Be safe, son," he said and then the hug was over.

Bubba blinked as he tried to process the emotions running through him. "I will, sir."

And then a knock sounded at the front door. Makenna. She hadn't officially resigned from her post yet, but she had agreed to drive him back to Fire Beach and spend a few days talking to the police department there and looking at rental properties.

"That will be Makenna. I love you guys, and I promise to come back soon."

✿

*M*akenna smiled as she glanced over at Bubba. The last few days with him had been amazing. He'd come with her to talk to every affected family and then let her cry on his shoulder when the emotions grew too heavy.

Kelsey had let him and his parents stay at her house until his parent's house was fixed, and Makenna had spent every evening there with him. They'd done devotions together and talked about their plans for the future. It had felt like a family, but now he was leaving, and she would hopefully be following soon.

She'd discussed her decision with Tad, and he had agreed to take the job if she resigned. That only left getting him trained and selling her small house if she decided Fire Beach was for her. She planned to do both after driving Bubba back to Fire Beach and spending a few days there. He'd said his friend Jordan might know of an opening in the force, and Cara had offered to let her stay at the bed and breakfast while she was in town. Makenna was excited but also nervous. Woodville had been her home for the last several years, and though it held a lot of bad memories, it held some good ones too. And she would miss it.

"You ready to be home?"

"Am I ever," he said. "It was nice to see my family, and I'm glad they're back in my life, but this is my home." He smiled as they passed the sign welcoming them to Fire Beach.

Makenna swallowed her nerves as she parked the car in front of Cara's bed and breakfast. Bubba had offered to get her settled before she took him home, but she was still a little nervous about staying with Cara. What if they didn't get along? What if she didn't fit in here?

She pushed the thoughts aside as she opened her door. That was fear talking, and fear was a liar. She would be fine. Things with Cara would be fine. She simply needed to trust that God's hand was in all of this.

Bubba rang the doorbell, but when no one answered, he turned the handle and opened the door. "She must be where she can't hear the bell," he said as he led the way inside. "Cara? It's Bubba and Makenna. Are you here?"

His voice echoed in the open room, and the hairs on the back of Makenna's neck stood up. Something felt wrong. She pulled her gun and motioned Bubba to let her lead the way. This wasn't her jurisdiction, but at least she was armed.

She cleared the current room and then followed the hallway to the right. The bedrooms lay to the left, so she assumed the kitchen and dining room would be the other direction. She wanted to clear those areas before opening bedroom doors.

As she stepped into the kitchen, the sound of moaning reached her ears. She quickly crossed the room, dropping to the floor when she spied Cara laying on the floor.

"Cara, are you okay?" Bubba had joined her and was carefully touching Cara's shoulder as Makenna pulled out her phone.

"This is Captain Makenna Drake of the Woodville police," she said when the 911 operator picked up. "I'm at Cara Hunter's bed and breakfast, and she's been injured. Please send an ambo and a local unit to 212 Whistler Avenue."

"Yes ma'am. I'm contacting them now. Please stay on the line until they arrive."

"What happened here?" Bubba asked as he looked up at her.

Makenna had no idea. What she did know was that the rest and relaxation she had been hoping for would have to wait. She may have just finished one case, but suddenly she found herself smack dab in the middle of another one.

Want to find out what happened to Cara? Be sure to read Secrets and Suspense.

The End!

IT'S NOT QUITE THE END!

❦

Thank you so much for reading *Never Forget the Past*. This book was inspired by my readers who told me Bubba needed his own story. Boy, did he ever, and now there are so many new characters to bring back around.

I hope you enjoyed the story as I really enjoyed writing it. If you did, would you do me a favor? If you did, please leave a review. It really helps. It doesn't have to be long - just a few words to help other readers know what they're getting.

I'd love to hear from you, not only about this story, but about the characters or stories you'd like read in the future. I'm always looking for new ideas and if I use one of your characters or stories, I'll send you a free ebook and paperback of the book with a special dedication. Write to me at loranahoopes@gmail.com. And if you'd like to see what's coming next, be sure to stop by authorloranahoopes.com

I also have a weekly newsletter that contains many wonderful things like pictures of my adorable children, chances to win awesome prizes, new releases and sales I might be holding, great books from other authors, and anything else that strikes my fancy and that I think you would enjoy. I'll even send you the first chapter of my newest (maybe not even released yet) book if you'd like to sign up.

Even better, I solemnly swear to only send out one newsletter a week (usually on Tuesday unless life gets in the way which with three kids it usually does). I will not spam you, sell your email address to solicitors or anyone else, or any of those other terrible things.

God Bless,
Lorana

NOT READY TO SAY GOODBYE YET?

*Y*our favorite characters from Fire Beach are never far away. Readers voted to read Cara's story next, so be prepared for ....

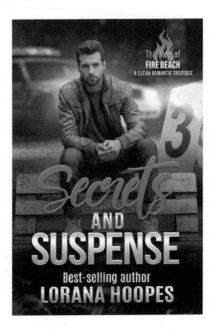

Secrets and Suspense

Bubba and Makenna found Cara on the floor...

She's ex-military...

What exactly is she hiding from her friends?

re-order Secrets and Suspense today!

A FREE STORY FOR YOU

*E*njoyed this story? Not ready to quit reading yet? If you sign up for my newsletter, you will receive The Billionaire's Impromptu Bet right away as my thank you gift for choosing to hang out with me.

The Billionaire's Impromptu Bet

A SWAT officer. A bored billionaire heiress. A bet that could change everything....

Read on for a taste of The Billionaire's Impromptu Bet....

THE BILLIONAIRE'S IMPROMPTU BET
PREVIEW

*B*rie Carter fell back spread eagle on her queen-sized canopy bed sending her blonde hair fanning out behind her. With a large sigh, she uttered, "I'm bored."

"How can you be bored? You have like millions of dollars." Her friend, Ariel, plopped down in a seated position on the bed beside her and flicked her raven hair off her shoulder. "You want to go shopping? I hear Tiffany's is having a special right now."

Brie rolled her eyes. Shopping? Where was the excitement in that? With her three platinum cards, she could go shopping whenever she wanted. "No, I'm bored with shopping too. I have everything. I want to do something exciting. Something we don't normally do."

Brie enjoyed being rich. She loved the unlimited

credit cards at her disposal, the constant apparel of new clothes, and of course the penthouse apartment her father paid for, but lately, she longed for something more fulfilling.

Ariel's hazel eyes widened. "I know. There's a new bar down on Franklin Street. Why don't we go play a little game?"

Brie sat up, intrigued at the secrecy and the twinkle in Ariel's eyes. "What kind of game?"

"A betting game. You let me pick out any man in the place. Then you try to get him to propose to you."

Brie wrinkled her nose. "But I don't want to get married." She loved her freedom and didn't want to share her penthouse with anyone, especially some man.

"You don't marry him, silly. You just get him to propose."

Brie bit her lip as she thought. It had been awhile since her last relationship and having a man dote on her for a month might be interesting, but.... "I don't know. It doesn't seem very nice."

"How about I sweeten the pot? If you win, I'll set you up on a date with my brother."

Brie cocked her head. Was she serious? The only thing Brie couldn't seem to buy in the world was the affection of Ariel's very handsome, very wealthy, brother. He was a movie star, just the kind of person Brie could consider marrying in the future. She'd had a crush on him as long as she and Ariel had been friends, but he'd always seen her as just that, his little sister's friend. "I thought you didn't want me dating your brother."

"I don't." Ariel shrugged. "But he's between girlfriends right now, and I know you've wanted it for ages. If you win this bet, I'll set you up. I can't guarantee any more than one date though. The rest will be up to you."

Brie wasn't worried about that. Charm she possessed in abundance. She simply needed some alone time with him, and she was certain she'd be able to convince him they were meant to be together. "All right. You've got a deal."

Ariel smiled. "Perfect. Let's get you changed then and see who the lucky man will be.

A tiny tug pulled on Brie's heart that this still wasn't right, but she dismissed it. This was simply a means to an end, and he'd never have to know.

🌺

*J*esse Calhoun relaxed as the rhythmic thudding of the speed bag reached his ears. Though he loved his job, it was stressful being the SWAT sniper. He hated having to take human lives and today had been especially rough. The team had been called out to a drug bust, and Jesse was forced to return fire at three hostiles. He didn't care that they fired at his team and himself first. Taking a life was always hard, and every one of them haunted his dreams.

"You gonna bust that one too?" His co-worker Brendan appeared by his side. Brendan was the opposite of Jesse in nearly every way. Where Jesse's hair was a dark copper, Brendan's was nearly black. Jesse sported paler skin and a dusting of freckles across his nose, but Brendan's skin was naturally dark and freckle free.

Jesse flashed a crooked grin, but kept his eyes on the small, swinging black bag. The speed bag was his way to release, but a few times he had started hitting while still too keyed up and he had ruptured the bag. Okay, five times, but who was counting really? Besides, it was a better way to calm his nerves than other things he could choose. Drinking, fights, gambling, women.

"Nah, I think this one will last a little longer." His shoulders began to burn, and he gave the bag another few punches for good measure before dropping his arms and letting it swing to a stop. "See? It lives to be hit at least another day." Every once in a while, Jesse missed training the way he used to. Before he joined the force, he had been an amateur boxer, on his way to being a pro, but a shoulder injury had delayed his training and forced him to consider something else. It had eventually healed, but by then he had lost his edge.

"Hey, why don't you come drink with us?" Brendan

clapped a hand on Jesse's shoulder as they headed into the locker room.

"You know I don't drink." Jesse often felt like the outsider of the team. While half of the six-man team was married, the other half found solace in empty bottles and meaningless relationships. Jesse understood that - their job was such that they never knew if they would come home night after night - but he still couldn't partake.

Brendan opened his locker and pulled out a clean shirt. He peeled off his current one and added deodorant before tugging on the new one. "You don't have to drink. Look, I won't drink either. Just come and hang out with us. You have no one waiting for you at home."

That wasn't entirely true. Jesse had Bugsy, his Boston Terrier, but he understood Brendan's point. Most days, Jesse went home, fed Bugsy, made dinner, and fell asleep watching TV on the couch. It wasn't much of a life. "All right, I'll go, but I'm not drinking."

Brendan's lips pulled back to reveal his perfectly white teeth. He bragged about them, but Jesse knew they were veneers. "That's the spirit. Hurry up and change. We don't want to leave the rest of the team waiting."

"Is everyone coming?" Jesse pulled out his shower necessities. Brendan might feel comfortable going out with just a new application of deodorant, but Jesse needed to wash more than just dirt and sweat off. He needed to wash the sound of the bullets and the sight of lifeless bodies from his mind.

"Yeah, Pat's wife is pregnant again and demanding some crazy food concoctions. Pat agreed to pick them up if she let him have an hour. Cam and Jared's wives are having a girls' night, so the whole gang can be together. It will be nice to hang out when we aren't worried about being shot at."

"Fine. Give me ten minutes. Unlike you, I like to clean up before I go out."

Brendan smirked. "I've never had any complaints. Besides, do you know how long it takes me to get my hair like this?"

Jesse shook his head as he walked into the shower, but he knew it was true. Brendan had rugged good looks and muscles to match. He rarely had a hard time finding a woman. Jesse on the other hand hadn't dated anyone in the last few months. It wasn't that he hadn't been looking, but he was quieter than his teammates. And he wasn't looking for right now. He was looking for forever. He just hadn't found it yet.

Click here to continue reading The Billionaire's Impromptu Bet.

THE STORY DOESN'T END!

You've met a few people and fallen in love....

I bet you're wondering how you can meet everyone else.

Star Lake Series:

When Love Returns: Can Presley and Brandon forget past hurts or will their stubborn natures keep them apart forever?

Once Upon a Star: Now that Blake has gained confidence and some muscle, will he finally be able to reveal his feelings to Audrey?

Love Conquers All: Now that Azarius has another chance with Laney, will he find the courage to share his life with her? Or will his emotional walls create a barrier that will leave him alone once more?

The Heartbeats Series:

Where It All Began: Will Sandra tell Henry her darkest secret? And will she ever be able to forgive herself and find healing? Find out in this emotional love story.

The Power of Prayer: Who will Callie choose and how will her choice affect the rest of her life? Find out in this touching novel.

When Hearts Collide: Amanda captivates his heart, but can Jared save her from making the biggest mistake of her life? A must read for mothers and daughters.

A Past Forgiven: Can Chad leave his bad-boy image behind and step up and be there for Jess and the baby?

Sweet Billionaires Series:

The Billionaire's Secret: Can Max really change his philandering ways? Or will one mistake seal his fate forever?

A Brush with a Billionaire: Will Brent and Sam's stubborn natures keep them apart or can a small town festival bring them together?

The Billionaire's Christmas Miracle: Drew Devonshire is captivated by the woman he meets at a masquerade ball, but who is she?

The Billionaire's Cowboy Groom: When Carrie returns to town requesting a divorce, can he convince her they belong together?

The Cowboy Billionaire: Coming Soon!

The Lawkeeper Series:

Lawfully Matched: Will Jesse find his fiancee's killer? And when Kate flies into his life, will he be able to put his painful past behind him in order to love again?

Lawfully Justified: Can Emma offer William a reason to stay? Can William find a way to heal from his broken past to start a future with Emma? Or will a haunting secret take away all the possibilities of this budding romance?

The Scarlet Wedding: William and Emma are planning their wedding, but an outbreak and a return from his past force them to change their plans. Is a happily ever after still in their future?

Lawfully Redeemed: Dani Higgins is a K9 cop looking to make a name for herself, but she finds herself at the mercy of a stranger after an accident. Calvin Phillips just wanted to help his brother, but somehow he ended up in the middle of a police investigation and caring for the woman trying to bring his brother in.

The Still Small Voice Series:

The Still Small Voice: Will Kat be able to give up control and do what God is asking of her?

A Spark in the Darkness coming soon!

Blushing Brides Series:

The Cowboy's Reality Bride: Laney Swann has been running from her past for years, but it takes meeting a man on a reality dating show to make her see there's no need to run.

The Reality Bride's Baby: Laney wants nothing more than a baby, but when she starts feeling dizzy is it pregnancy or something more serious?

The Producer's Unlikely Bride: Ava McDermott is waiting for the perfect love, but after agreeing to a fake relationship with Justin, she finds herself falling for real.

Ava's Blessing in Disguise: Five years after marriage, Ava faces a mysterious illness that threatens to ruin her career. Will she find out what it is?

The Soldier's Steadfast Bride: coming soon

The Men of Fire Beach

Fire Games: Cassidy returns home from Who Wants to Marry a Cowboy to find obsessive letters from a fan. The cop assigned to help her wants to get back to his case, but what she sees at a fire may just be the key he's looking for.

Lost Memories and New Beginnings: She has no idea who she is. He's the doctor caring for her. When her past collides with his present, can he keep her safe?

When Questions Abound A companion story to Lost Memories, this book tells the story from Detective Jordan Graves's point of view.

Never Forget the Past

Secrets and Suspense coming soon!

Stand Alones:

Love Renewed: This books is part of the multi author second chance series. When fate reunites high school sweethearts separated by life's choices, can they find a second chance at love at a snowy lodge amid a little mystery?

Her children's early reader chapter book series:

The Wishing Stone #1: Dangerous Dinosaur

The Wishing Stone #2: Dragon Dilemma

The Wishing Stone #3: Mesmerizing Mermaids

The Wishing Stone #4: Pyramid Puzzle

The Wishing Stone Inspirations 1: Mary's Miracle

To see a list of all her books

authorloranahoopes.com

loranahoopes@gmail.com

DISCUSSION QUESTIONS

1. What was your favorite scene in the book? What made it your favorite?

2. Did you have a favorite line in the book? What do you think made it so memorable?

3. Who was your favorite character in the book and why?

4. Where you surprised by any of the events?

5. What do you think would be the hardest part about taking on a new identity?

6. What did you learn about God from reading this book?

7. How can you use that knowledge in your life from now on?

8. What can you take away from Bubba's and Makenna's relationship?

9. What do you think would make the story even better?

ABOUT THE AUTHOR

Lorana Hoopes is an inspirational author originally from Texas but now living in the PNW with her husband and three children. When not writing, she can be seen kickboxing at the gym, singing, or acting on stage. One day, she hopes to retire from teaching and write full time.